Embers of the Day

Rosemary J. Kind

Printed in the United Kingdom

First Printing, 2018 Alfie Dog Limited

The author can be found at: authors@alfiedog.com

Cover image: Alfie Dog Limited

ISBN 978-1-909894-41-9

Published by
Alfie Dog Limited
Rose Bank, Norton Lindsey,
Warwickshire, CV35 8JQ
Tel: 07712 647754

DEDICATION

To my office co-workers,
Alfie, Shadow, Aristotle and Wilma
thank you for all your help and support

CONTENTS

EMBERS OF THE DAY

"Stop fussing, Freda. Let the boy come in." Papa lay back against the pillows wheezing, even to him, his skin looked paper thin, his frail hand reaching across the bedspread, quilted by his wife all those years ago. He remembered its many blue and white pieces and the hours it took her to stitch it, in the early years of their marriage. The breeze from the open window was a welcome sensation across his face.

"But you heard what the doctor said, Papa, you need to rest." Freda tidied the covers of her father's bed and took his hand. It was hard to see her father like this; he had been such a strong support for her over the last few years. Even since the old man's eyesight had failed, he hadn't stopped taking care of the family.

Papa turned towards her and taking her hand in both of his said, "Freda, my time has come, we both know that rest isn't going to make any difference. Let the boy come. Let him brighten the final hours of an old man's life." Papa was prepared for what lay ahead. The thought of death didn't frighten him. He was tired. He would be reunited with Anya, but he feared for those he left behind.

Freda knew there was no point in arguing, in truth, her father was right, but she didn't want to believe that the end was so close.

The late spring sun beat down on the farmland that stretched around the house on all sides. She could see men working in the distance. The farm was never idle, Freda thought, as she went out to call her son. This was a lovely time of year in northern Italy and even now, the intensity of the light accentuated the range of colours around the courtyard; the brown stone, the green leaves, and the bright flowers in tubs by the doors.

"Pedro," Freda called, "Pedro."

The innocent brown eyes poked out from around the stable door, "Mama," Pedro replied excitedly, "the mare has had her foal. Come and see."

Pedro took Freda's hand and led her into the stable. Pedro kept the stable clean and tidy, but the gentle smell of the animals hung in the air. A tiny foal struggled to remain upright on legs that wobbled awkwardly on the hay. The foal's mother stood watching protectively as Freda put her hands on Pedro's shoulders. "That's wonderful darling, she's doing well." Freda hesitated, "Papa is asking for you," she said gently.

"Can I go to him?" Pedro's face lit up with excitement. He loved his grandfather. It was Papa who'd taught him to fish and to draw. It was Papa who'd brought home Snuffles. Snuffles was a scruffy little mongrel of a dog, with the sort of face that made you want to take care of him and Pedro had. It was Papa who'd sat Pedro on his knee and told him about the old times on the farm. It was Papa who'd shown Pedro how to train Snuffles to obey his every command and it was Papa who Pedro went to when he was frightened or worried. Papa had been not just a grandfather but the father he had never known. Pedro had been only six months old when his father died and his mother moved them back to live with her own father. Now he was nearly eleven and he knew that soon Papa would be gone too. He'd heard his mother talking to the doctor and although

Pedro dreaded the day that Papa would be gone, he knew he had to be brave.

"Don't spend too long with him, Pedro. The doctor says he needs to rest." Even now, whatever her eyes told her, Freda didn't want to believe there was no hope.

Pedro ran across the courtyard to the house, the warm breeze giving his curly hair a tousled look, while the scents of the early summer washed over him with a quite unfounded hope. His grandfather had many dark days as his illness had progressed. There had been days when he had been too weak and in too much pain to allow Pedro to sit with him. On his good days, Pedro would sit with him and tell him everything he'd seen and all that he'd done. Sometimes he would simply sit near his grandfather and draw, describing what he drew as he went along. Pedro loved the times he could spend with the old man, even though he was now so weak. For a boy so young, Pedro had done a lot of growing up. It was hard to mourn for a father you'd never known, but he knew how much he wished his father was alive. When the other boys talked about playing football with their fathers, or told of their fathers reading to them, Pedro remained silent. He was more familiar with loss than most children of his age were, but with his grandfather's help, he learnt to carry his burden without it taking away the joy of his youth. His grandfather had taught him to honour the dead by continuing to live. To build on the legacy he had been left and savour the little pleasures in life. It was a lesson well learnt in one so young.

"Papa," said Pedro quietly, as he entered his grandfather's bedroom. Pedro saw the Bible lying on the bedside table and knew it must have been his mother reading from it. A bee flew across the open window, stopping briefly but not coming in.

"Pedro," said Papa, holding out his hand. "Come child, be my eyes." The last two years since his eyesight had failed had been so hard for Papa to accept. He loved the world around him and missed seeing the changing of the seasons on the farm. "Tell me what you see."

"I saw the foal stand Papa. She's all wobbly and can't walk far without falling over, but she stood. It was amazing. Her mother is so gentle with her, but she still lets her fall over and get up on her own."

"What colour is she Pedro? What does she look like?" The hours that Papa had spent teaching Pedro to draw had paid such dividends these last two years. Papa had taught Pedro to look at the things around him properly, to see what was really there and not just to take a superficial glance at the world around him. He'd taught Pedro that to be a great artist he must see the detail, the difference between light and shade, the true lines of the world and not the corrected image that the mind presented if you didn't keep control.

"Buildings are like life," Papa would say, "they never have straight lines and perfect corners, their roofs have twists and curves, their stonework is never even."

Pedro knew how to look for the little variations that others so easily missed.

"She's the most beautiful dapple grey, with hazel eyes and the softest hair. The grey is uneven with flecks of white. When I look at her coat, I can see all sorts of patterns in the colours. It's like seeing the patterns in the flames of the fire. She's wonderful Papa."

"And at the window, Pedro, what do you see?"

Pedro let go of his grandfather's hand and went over to the window.

"Tell me as though you are going to draw it Pedro. What

do you see?"

"I see green shoots in the field, Papa. They are waving gently in the wind. There are some places where the shoots are very small and look as though they're struggling to come through. In between the shoots, I can still see brown earth where the field was ploughed. The ploughman did well; the lines are almost straight. They are straight as a hand drawn line is straight and not as a ruler would be. The hedge is a darker green and I can see the vines on the hillside beyond. The sky is deep blue, but the colour is lighter as you look to the horizon, Papa and there are no clouds anywhere. Not even the fine strands that seem so very high up and make the sky look paler. The shadow of the hedge is quite small."

"That's because it's nearly lunchtime, Pedro, the sun is high."

"I know, Papa," said Pedro excitedly. "You taught me how the shadows change as the sun moves across the sky. You showed me how they grow shorter and then longer again as the day goes on."

"What else can you see, Pedro? Is the wisteria still out in the courtyard?"

"There are still a few flowers Papa. They look more white than purple as though the sun has faded them. Most of the flowers have died. They are brown and crumpled, dried by the sun." Pedro turned from the window towards his grandfather as though the very word of death had broken the spell of the beautiful day. "Are you going to die, Papa?" Pedro asked, his voice trembling.

"Yes, child, it's almost time for me to go with the wisteria. It's time for me to join the old family, time to make way for new growth. I've lived a long and happy life Pedro, it's right that I should move on."

"Why do things have to die Papa?" Pedro returned to his grandfather's bedside and his grandfather reached up to touch his tears.

"It's part of the cycle of life, Pedro, the part of the plant that is old and withered must die away to make room for the new growth. Each year the wisteria grows back, beautiful new blooms on the old wood from last year. The old wood hasn't gone away, it's what gives strength to the plant, enabling it to keep growing. And so it is with people, the new generation must take their strength from the old ones. The young build on strength of the old. For two years, you have been my eyes Pedro and together we have seen many things. Now it's time for you to go on and live for me, as I can no longer do that either. Take care of your Mama, Pedro. She's going to need you to be the man of the house now, child. In the same way that you have been my eyes, now you must be the eyes for your Mama."

"But Mama can see," said Pedro confused.

"Everyone can look, Pedro, but not many can see. Be there to see what is real for her. Help her see light when she can only see darkness, help her to see colour when the world seems black and white. There are many ways in which we can be eyes for those we love; your Mama will need you, Pedro. I am tired, I must rest now child." Papa gently touched Pedro's cheek then brought his hand down to his side on the bed. Pedro moved away towards the door, tears rolling down his face. His grandfather's message was confusing. He slipped back out to the courtyard and sat at the bottom of the wisteria looking up into its branches, Snuffles sitting beside him, nuzzling his hands. He watched the greens and pale purple seem to change their colour as the sun moved round. He watched the bees coming to the open flowers and taking pollen; he saw how they rubbed their back legs against the flowers to pick up the pollen for carrying before moving away again and others taking their place. He watched as the sun was beginning to sink lower in the sky, appearing to become a richer orange as it did so. He thought of the sunset he had drawn for his grandfather with the colours of burning embers crossing the sky. He thought too of the morning that he and Papa had woken early and gone out into the field to watch the sunrise. Beginnings and endings, endings and beginnings, a never ending wheel turning from one to the other.

He was still sitting beneath the wisteria when the shadows had lengthened and he heard his mother's crying from the window above. Pedro knew then that the time had come for his grandfather to go to the place the old wisteria flowers had gone and that it was time for him to take care of his mother. Pedro had thought a lot about his grandfather's words and he knew he must give his mother hope and comfort. Together they must see the colour that his grandfather had left behind, his legacy to both of them.

When his mother came out into the courtyard to find Pedro, he went to her and said, "Papa can see again now. The wisteria flowers are still purple where Papa is. The sky will always be blue and there will be no more darkness for him."

Freda ran her hand through Pedro's hair as she held him to her. Through her own tears, she smiled seeing how much of the old man still stood before her in the shape of her son.

Then Pedro said, "Can we take a cutting from the wisteria in the courtyard and plant it on Papa's grave, so that it will flower there every year? Purple is such a lovely colour."

THE PERFECT CRIME

"Laura, thanks for looking after my little darlings while I was away."

"Don't mention it, the pleasure was all mine." I smiled down the phone. If only Rebecca knew what I'd done.

"I was quite worried about you before I went. You seemed very low. Is there anything I can do?"

"I'm fine now. Really I am and believe me when I say I appreciate everything you've already done." Every little thing! I grinned.

"Well if you're sure. I'll see you next week."

"Yes, bye." I put the phone down and nodded to myself, yes I was fine.

#

"Are you coming? We're already late." Matthew shouted up the stairs to me. I could hear the irritation resonating in his voice.

"Oh will you just lay off. We've got plenty of time." I bit my lip rather than say any more.

"You may not mind if we miss the train, but I need to get to London. You either come now or you can make your own way to the station."

I mimicked him under my breath but out loud I said "That would hardly be sensible. We're travelling on the same train. I'll be five minutes and you 'can' afford to wait." I went into the bathroom and looked at the last spare needle from my IVF treatment. Could I go through with this? Did I still love Matthew? The injustice was too much for any woman to bear. I still wanted children, I would never come to terms with the fact that I couldn't and now he wanted to leave me for a younger version.

"You said five minutes, have you seen the time?"

"All right, I'm coming." I picked up my book and briefcase and headed along the landing. Deep breath, final check, yes, everything was in place. I breezed downstairs. "What are you so worked up about, it's only ten past?" I looked at the grandfather clock.

"It's slow." He tapped his own watch and thrust it towards me. "See."

I didn't want an argument, today of all days. We drove in silence.

Once we were on the train, I took out my book. He hid behind a broadsheet newspaper. After ten minutes he put it down. "Have you thought about the question I asked you?"

I sat up in disbelief; surely he wasn't going to raise the question of divorce on a crowded morning train. "What question?" He hadn't raised it for weeks. Of course, I knew he was still seeing the other woman, but my refusal to divorce him had seemed to stop him in his tracks. We had separate bedrooms now, but other than that, things had achieved a new normal. I'd expected him to leave, but I knew he wanted the house. Well he would just have to want, because Laura Wilbright didn't lose.

"You know what question. The 'D' word."

I gritted my teeth and tried to keep my composure, speaking as clearly as I could despite the wobble in my voice. There was no turning back now. "Let's get this straight and perhaps the whole carriage would like to express a view. The IVF hasn't worked. We can't have children. You want a male heir, so now you want to divorce me?"

"It's not like that at all. Please!"

"So how is it exactly?" Even I could hear the sarcasm in my tone. I was pleased to find that he raised his newspaper and didn't answer. Everyone around the carriage stared in another direction.

Nobody tells me how to live my life and nobody demands a divorce from me either. It wasn't my fault I couldn't have children. There was no way I was going to let Matthew abandon me so that he could 'have the chance to have children with somebody else'. How dare he? He had married me 'for better or worse' and as far as I was concerned, 'til death us do part' was the end of the matter.

He put the paper down again. "It's that job. All you do is work."

"Hello, this is kettle calling pot. Come in, pot. How exactly would we have afforded the house if I hadn't worked? Besides, what else was I supposed to do? You know I'd be a mother if I could."

I thought back to the early days of our marriage, when he seemed to love me for who I was. Maybe Matthew hadn't changed. Maybe all he'd ever seen me as was the means to produce a son. I looked out at the blue sky with the clouds scudding past. Not a bad day for a new beginning.

The paper went down and I prepared for the next sniper fire. "It isn't even as though you've got a proper job."

I took a deep breath to mask the gasp. Even I wasn't expecting that one. "What's that supposed to mean?"

"Well, look at you in your combat trousers. It's hardly professional attire is it?"

"So just because I don't wear a suit, I haven't got a career. No one in marketing wears suits, besides the pockets come in handy." I smiled. "I don't know why I let you talk me into travelling together. It was a stupid idea."

"Well at least we're on different trains coming home." He went back to his paper, rustling it into place with a real flourish.

I'd booked the train tickets as I always did, part of the joys of a family business. Not that there was a family to pass it onto. There'd be no next generation 'Wilbright and sons', not with me anyway.

The last straw had been the miscarriage. The baby was nearly five months old when we lost it. The nurse said, "I'm sorry but you've lost your little girl." I was distraught, but Matthew's response was both amazing and repulsive.

"Girl," he replied. "I don't want a girl. I want a son." Then he'd walked out of the hospital, leaving me to grieve alone.

I looked across at him now and felt nothing. I strengthened my resolve, how had I ever loved this man. I'd never really known him until recently and now that I did, I didn't like what I saw.

"Where are you heading to?" Asked Matthew as the train rolled into St Pancras.

"Victoria Embankment."

"I'll leave you here then. See you tonight." He sounded relieved.

"Yes, bye." I was conscious of the CCTV cameras around me. Normally, I barely remembered they were there, it had been so important to think through how they would see me at each stage of the day. It was for the sake of the cameras that I needed two disguises. For now, it was important to be Laura Wilbright, the marketing executive and wife of Matthew, easily recognisable and seen in all the right places. The disguises would come later.

The day whizzed by. "Well that concludes the meeting.

Laura, are you off immediately or do you need an office?"

I looked at my watch, 15.00. Being early wasn't an option today. "An office would be great, Geoff, thanks." It was impossible to concentrate on anything other than running through the last minute preparations. I was clear on when I had to change outfit and what I needed to put where. I would have to carry all my accessories with me. A discovered wig or piece of trousers could be enough for the whole plot to unravel. I had contrived to make the baggage part of the disguise. I did a final time-check and synchronised my watch with the radio controlled one on the wall of the office, 17.05, time to go. Time was crucial with only minutes between each train connection.

I reached the Blackfriars Thameslink platform at 17.22, boarded the train and chose a seat, carefully checking until I found one next to a man whose seat was reserved as far as Bedford. He looked as though he would be eager to talk to an attractive woman. Bedford was the last stop for this train and I could change there to my connecting, home bound, train.

"Do you mind if I sit here?" I asked, with a smile.

"Yes. I mean no, certainly." The man nervously moved his coat over a little.

I slipped off my coat and put it on the luggage rack, opened my briefcase and took out the two plastic bags and my book, before putting the briefcase with my coat.

I eased into my seat, and with all the silky charm I could muster said, "Don't you just hate London. I always feel so good to get away."

"Yes, I'm never sorry to leave."

"Do you travel into London often?" I had only a few minutes to exchange business cards, for my alibi to carry weight.

"Yes I work here," he said, still seeming surprised that I was talking to him.

Now was my opportunity, "I'm Laura, Laura Wilbright." I fished out a card from my pocket, "I'm a marketing consultant based in Leicester. What do you do?" As he took my card, I held my breath; I needed him to return the favour. I must obtain his contact details and have proof that I was here.

"Trevor," he said in reply, "Trevor Harris. I'm a financial analyst." He started searching his pockets and eventually produced a rather tatty card, which he gave to me.

I relaxed a little and checked my watch, 17.29. I still had seven minutes before the train stopped at Kings Cross. I opened my book and made a play of reading a page, before turning to Trevor and saying "I'm just going to check if my friend joined this train. Would you mind saving my seat for me?" I flashed Trevor another smile, got up and turned my book over with the pages splayed out on the seat.

"No, of course, see you in a while." Trevor was already putty in my hands.

I picked up the two bags and headed along to the next carriage. I placed the bag with the spare clothes carefully and neatly on the luggage rack for later. The trick had been to buy two of each item of clothing to cover all eventualities. It would be quicker to change trousers than reassemble the multi-season combat trousers, with their legs that each zipped off at two different levels.

I took the second bag to the nearest toilet. There was no one outside to see Laura Wilbright enter the toilet and no one outside to see me emerge with spiky black hair, sunglasses, heavy shoes, three quarter length trousers and a short-sleeved t-shirt, with a low cut, scooped neckline, barely concealing a large bust, with the extra padding I had added. In the combat pockets, I had stashed the remaining props for my second disguise. In a separate pocket designed for a mobile phone, was the discreetly hidden syringe.

Researching poisons had been quite difficult, but without doubt, the hardest part had been obtaining the poison that would be most effective. Even now, I wondered if it was as potent as everything I'd read indicated. Matthew was never ill. In all the years I'd known him, he'd maybe missed one or two days' work at most. Perhaps he would be the one person who could resist such extreme poison. It was a risk I had to take. Now wasn't the time to have doubts. If South American tribes could do it, let alone Russian spies, then so could I.

Having a friend that kept frogs for a hobby was a distinct advantage, but normally when they're kept in captivity, the food given to the Poison Dart Frog isn't sufficiently toxic to cause them to generate poison. It had taken a lot of cultivating my friendship with Rebecca for her to trust me enough to look after the frogs, whilst she went to Peru for three weeks. It had taken more painstaking research to work out what to feed them to produce poison. After that, I still had to find a way of causing them enough stress to release the poison so that I could collect it without personal harm. It had taken me hours of chasing them round their tank with a stick to have the desired effect. The needle for the injection had been the easy part; the IVF treatment had been my last hope of conceiving. Then it was me suffering the discomfort of injections. Now it was Matthew's turn to feel the pain; in the circumstances, the irony appealed to me.

As the train pulled into Kings Cross, I knew there was no going back. I'd worked so hard to get this right. There was only one train from St Pancras Station, at this time of day, that gave enough time to switch back to the slower Blackfriars to Bedford train, and that was the one for which Matthew's ticket was booked.

It was time to be seen on closed circuit television again. This time as someone who looked quite different from Laura. It was vital that I got this part right, for my alibi to be secure. My watch showed that we were running one minute late as I got off the train. It was now 17.37. I had eight minutes to get from King's Cross Station to the train at St Pancras. I slipped through every gap in the flow of people and quickly followed the walkway to the other station. I looked up at the screens showing the departing trains. They said platform 4 for the 17.45. I guessed that Matthew would already be on board, but looking for him would not be difficult. I'd made the reservation, Coach B, seat 22. For the return journey I had deliberately chosen a single seat to allow him to spread out without annoying anyone.

My watch said 17.43 as I got onto the train at coach F. I went into the toilet and made a final check on my appearance. Was there a risk of Matthew recognising me?

I couldn't be certain which way round the carriage seats were facing and whether I would be approaching him face on, or from behind. With the appearance changes I should be safe. The enlarged bust should do the trick anyway. After all, Matthew was just like most men, if he saw a low neckline, he would never look as far as the face.

The whistle blew as I came out of the toilet and went to find a seat in a neighbouring carriage. There were 24 minutes before I would get off the train. Timing was everything. Suddenly I realised I wasn't certain what Matthew had been wearing that morning. I'd been so busy with my own preparations I hadn't really looked at him. The last time I was going to see my husband alive and I hadn't even looked at him. What a state things had got to.

I planned to make my move at around 18.00. The poison would take a few minutes to act, by which time I should be off the train. As long as the needle pierced the skin it would be effective. I didn't need to push it all the way in, tempting as that was. Once again, it was going to be important to be seen by the right people, in my current disguise.

At 17.59, I got up and started making my way towards carriage B. At the start of the carriage I checked the syringe was ready and then set off. I checked the seat numbers. I was at the high end. The low numbered seats at the far end were facing away from me. I could relax a little. I moved slowly, to make sure that the lurching of the train didn't make me lose my footing. I couldn't afford any accidents. I also needed to be able to pick out Matthew and check he was alone. Yes, there he was, his sandy hair showing on the edge of the headrest and his old linen jacket resting on the arm of the chair. The plan was to lurch with the train as I got to his place and administer the syringe through the hip level pocket of my trousers, into his arm, in the mêlée. I would then make a show of apologising to make sure that someone saw the woman with spiky black hair and then move away as quickly as possible, before anyone had chance to talk to me and delay my progress.

I was at seat 34. There was no time for any last minute doubts. This was it. I made the last few steps and lurched. There, it was done.

"Sorry!" I said in a loud, thick voice. "So sorry." I didn't look into the man's face, but patted his arm as I said sorry again and then moved on as though embarrassed. At least one person had turned and looked at me; I hoped it would be enough. I had a further four minutes before leaving the train. The toilet of that carriage had someone waiting outside, so I carried on to the one at the end. Fortunately, there was no one around as I slipped inside. I quickly changed the black wig, for a slightly longer blonde one, reduced the size of my bust by removing the padding, put on ordinary glasses instead of the sunglasses, removed the t-shirt to reveal an even skinnier one with shoestring straps and unzipped the remaining removable section of trousers to leave shorts. Then I slipped off the overshoes to reveal very simple flat pumps. I packed all the spare items into the handy, roll-up backpack that was stashed in one of the pockets and put the rucksack on my back. Once again the new look was complete. The person who had accidentally stumbled in carriage 'B' would not be seen leaving the train.

It was 18.08 and the train was pulling into Luton as I came out of the toilets and stood at the door ready to get off. There was no time to waste to make sure my alibi was complete. At 18.09, I stepped off the St Pancras train and checked the board for the incoming 18.13. It was still running roughly on time and I had no difficulty in getting myself ready to get on. I counted the carriages carefully as the train pulled in and was ready to get in at the door by the correct luggage rack. Yes, it was still there. The bag I'd left neatly, before leaving the train earlier, was still on its own, on the top luggage rack. I took it down and went into the toilet. With new trousers, elegant court shoes, no glasses or wig and with the layering of t-shirts and jumper replaced, Laura Wilbright was back. I looked exactly as I had before I left the train 37 minutes ago. I walked calmly back to the seat Trevor was holding for me and picked up my book to sit down.

"I'm sorry," I said, "You must think me very rude. I've

been ages. It took me a long time to get through all the people sitting in the aisles from here to the end of the train and back. After all that, my friend wasn't there." I beamed him another smile.

"No problem," said Trevor, melting under my gaze. "We're nearly at Bedford now anyway. You'll have to change here, if you want the Leicester train."

"Oh yes," I said, "thank you."

I packed my things back into my briefcase and settled down to read my book for the remaining part of the journey. It was 18.38 when the train pulled in to Bedford, giving me a quarter of an hour to waste before my connecting train to Leicester. I went into the station café for a coffee.

It had been amazing that on this day of all days, all the trains had run on time. I climbed aboard the 18.54 for the final leg of my journey. I began to think about how everything would play out later. I presumed I would get home and then at some point the police would call to tell me the tragic news that my husband had died. I wondered if it would be put down as natural causes or if there would be any suspicion of foul play. The beauty of the symptoms caused by the Poison Dart Frog is that the real reason for death is unlikely to be obvious; the heart is such a delicate organ. Matthew didn't have a history of heart problems, but he had a lot of stress in his life, it wasn't difficult to accept a heart attack as the cause of death. I checked that Trevor's card was safely in my pocket. It was so important to have an alibi, and after all, I had been on the Blackfriars to Bedford train when it happened.

My train pulled in to Leicester at 19.38 and having travelled with Matthew to the station that morning I didn't have a car. I went to get a taxi home. As I sat in the back of the cab, I began thinking about how I should play the grief-stricken widow. I needed to appear shocked, but mustn't overdo it. I wasn't usually an outwardly emotional person; this wasn't the time to behave out of character. There was no reason to give anyone a cause for concern by being too theatrical, not after everything had gone so well.

The taxi journey didn't take long in an evening and it was still only 20.00 as the taxi stopped on the empty drive.

"That'll be £9.00, luv," the driver said.

I flinched at being called 'love' but said nothing. I found some bank notes folded up in my purse and handed over a tenner. "Keep the change."

"Thanks, luv," said the driver before heading off into the night.

I found my key, took a deep breath and went into the house to begin the rest of my life. Free at last from the constraints of being married to Matthew. He may have been the one asking for a divorce, but putting up with him hadn't been plain sailing either. I'd kept my promise 'til death us do part'. There was to be no ignominy of divorce for me and no children for him. I closed the front door behind me, put down my briefcase, lent back against the closed door and sighed.

"Laura, is that you?"

"Matthew!"

He came down the stairs with a suitcase in his hand. "It's better like this, much cleaner than leaving you a note."

I barely managed to control my voice. I was stunned. It felt as though I had been slapped hard across the face. "But! Where's your car?" My head was spinning. Thoughts seemed to come at me from all directions. If Matthew was here what had gone wrong? The poison couldn't have been strong enough. Maybe the frogs hadn't been sufficiently stressed for it to work. Perhaps Matthew had been strong enough to survive the poison. Had he realised it was me? I felt faint and moved to sit on the chair in the hall before I could fall down. My heart raced. I had no idea what to say. Should I confess? It struck me that Matthew seemed oblivious to my discomfiture.

"Whenever I went it was always going to be a shock," Matthew continued confidently, as though he had planned what he was going to say. "Carol has just taken the first load of my stuff, whilst I packed the rest. She'll be back for me in a few minutes. I've decided some things are more important than houses. You can keep it. I want to be with Carol whether I'm divorced from you or not."

"When did you get back?" I was numb, feeling my whole life unravel. "The train?" I found it difficult to be coherent.

"It's been a strange day. I didn't go to a meeting at the office today. I lied to you. I went to collect a ring that I'd bought for Carol."

"How long have you been back?" I asked weakly, trying to piece together the events of the day that I had felt completely in control of five minutes earlier. "Is that a new suit?" I looked at him properly for the first time that day. I was vaguely aware that he looked different.

"Yes. I decided it was time for a new start all round. The funniest thing happened when I took my old suit into a charity shop near St Pancras. Whilst I was in the shop there was someone asking if they had any suits in his size. Strangely, he was exactly the same size as me."

"Who was he?" I asked, panic-stricken.

"Just some chap who needed a suit for his sister's wedding in Sheffield tomorrow. It was funny, he even looked a bit like me. I told him he might as well have my train ticket as well, if he didn't mind waiting until the 17.45.

At least it would get him most of the way to Sheffield and he would only have to pay the last leg from Leicester. The ticket was no use to me, I needed to get back to do my packing and it was only 12.30 at the time. So now I'm leaving and you'll be hearing from my solicitor. I still want a divorce, however long you make me wait. Goodbye, Laura."

I was speechless. What could I say? I couldn't tell him what I'd done. I certainly didn't feel euphoric any more. This was it. This was my future. Not only was I a killer but a childless killer with a failed marriage. What had I done? "Goodbye Matthew." I slumped down onto the floor of the hall, staring into space.

CORDON BLEU GOO

'Stupid old witch. You know we all hate you.' I looked around guiltily to see if anyone had realised what I was thinking. I caught sight of my sunken sponge cake. There was overly runny butter icing seeping out of the middle where a piece had been cut for judging. The heat in the tent certainly wasn't helping. Next to it stood Joan's perfectly bronzed fruit cake and Pam's fruit scones. Both of their creations always seemed to be placed in the show. I turned away seeing Joan, the other side of the tent as I did so. She was smiling at the head judge. Rumour had it that there was a new judging panel, but the names of the other judges had been shrouded in secrecy.

"Oh, Elizabeth, how good to see you again this year. A rather fine display don't you think? Now which one of those lovely offerings is yours? Not the fruit cake is it?"

'You've known me fifteen years you condescending old woman, you know it's not the fruit cake.' Oh, if only I could bring myself to say it. I had no idea why I played this game each year, except that I was expected to, and Brian so wanted me to fit in. "No, Edith." I forced a smile. "I think we all know who's that is. Have you entered your jam again?"

It was all part of the game. Of course Edith had entered her jam. She always entered her jam and she always won.

I couldn't help thinking that, even after all these years, moving to the country had been a mistake. These were things you had to be brought up to, not things you could suddenly become good at. What self-respecting city girl spent her spare time quilting, lace making and cooking? After all, what was Marks and Spencer's for?

It had all been Brian's idea. 'Let's move to the country and get a smallholding.' Well it was all very well for him wanting to play 'The Good Life', but I missed feeling at home amongst Gucci handbags. I'd never been a jeans and tee shirt person, let alone long skirts and cotton blouses.

"Elizabeth." I cringed as I heard the drawn-out pronunciation of my name by Joan. "I think the judging is about to be announced. Are we excited about the results this year?"

'I don't know, are we?' Went through my head, but then I said, "Hello Joan, excited as ever." I almost thought I should slap my thigh for emphasis, but maybe that would be going a bit far.

"Of course I hear there's a new class this year with all the cakes being considered for a special prize."

I withered beneath her knowing look. "Oh, that is exciting, Joan." If only I had the courage to add my real feelings. 'I'm always delighted to have more opportunities to fail.'

There were 'shhing' noises around the marquee as the head judge came to the stand. I looked round at the gathered crowd and noticed my grandson, Peter, holding his thumbs up to me. If only he knew just how bad a cook his grandmother was, still he was only seven, thankfully at the age where I'm wonderful in his eyes. Then I spotted nine-year-old Timothy grinning at me and I started to get a feeling that something was going on.

"Ladies and Gentlemen, it has been our pleasure to judge this year's Buckleby fete and I have to say that we have been astounded by the entries this year..."

I let my concentration go and started looking for Brian. Why wasn't he with the boys? He was supposed to be taking them round the animals while the boring judging was going on, but there was no sign of him anywhere. I automatically joined in the applause as the judge announced the result of the best dahlias. I wished it were one of those shows where the head judge placed the results against the exhibits, for all to admire, rather than her laboriously announcing each category. Then I caught sight of Brian through the opening of the marquee; he was just coming out of the beer tent. If Brian was there, who was with Peter and Timothy? I started to make my way through the crowd to where I'd last seen them. "Excuse me. Sorry. Could I just squeeze... Oh was that your foot? I'm so sorry."

"Shhh."

"And now we move on to the culinary delights that Buckleby had in store for us this year. Thanks to a suggestion from one of our younger visitors..."

I gasped as I saw Timothy, together with Joan's granddaughter and another youngster I didn't recognise bundled forwards to stand alongside the judge. "...we decided to put the cakes in all the different categories head to head in the 'taste test'. With the help of these special judges, all the cakes have been sampled and we have here the results together with the judges' comments. In third place we have the jam tarts made by Edith Cresswell, with her own jam. Hang on, I just need to put my glasses on to read the children's comments... 'they were really nice and there was lots of jam' 'strawberry jam's my favourite' and 'I thought they looked really pretty'. Well Edith, those comments take some beating. In second place we have Joan Thomas's fruit cake..."

There was a ripple of excitement around the tent. Joan hadn't won, she was only second. That had never happened before. I looked back to where she was a few minutes earlier to see Joan forcing a smile that was obviously fake.

The head of judging continued unperturbed. "The judges said, 'it was a yummy cake', 'there was lots of fruit' and 'I like the cherry bits best'. Finally, we come to our winner. I think I'm right in saying she has never won a prize in the show before. This year's first prize goes to Elizabeth Hunter." There was loud applause as I put my hands to my face and shook my head slightly in disbelief.

The head judge held her hand up for quiet. "I think it's important that we should hear the judges' comments." The marquee became silent. "'It was really nice and gooey', 'I though the icing was best' and finally 'can I have another piece, it's scrummy'." A cheer went up and I felt hands pushing me forwards through the crowd as I went to collect my certificate. I smiled at Joan who glared back.

As I came away, I found Brian standing with Timothy and Peter.

"You see Gran," said Peter, "I always said you were the best."

I took Peter and Timothy by the hand and smiled at Brian. I may not feel quite at home in the country, but I can hold my own as a granny with the best of them. What more could any grandmother ask for?

HER MAJESTY'S PLEASURE

"Does the defendant have anything to say?" The judge looked down sternly from the bench.

It seemed a big courtroom for such a trivial case. Now was my chance to speak. "Yes I do. I prefer to think of my actions as the natural consequence of the need for redistribution and therefore perfectly justifiable. I really don't think this case should be viewed as a crime and therefore, I can't possibly be guilty."

'His Honour' didn't agree and I'm now at the start of a three year sentence at Her Majesty's pleasure. I'm not sure that Her Majesty would regard it as a 'pleasure'; not given this poky cell that smells like it hasn't seen a can of Pledge in its life. The furniture's seen better days, and don't get me started on my 'en suite' facilities. Like it or not, it's home, at least until I can get the appeal judge to see sense.

What would you have done in my shoes? To all intents and purposes, we were the same, or we should've been. We lived next door to each other, in similar houses. You know the type, four bedroom estate houses, double garage, no character. Sheila's house looked just like ours, from the outside anyway. That was where the similarity ended. Hers was paid for and mine was mortgaged to the rooftop. She had a good job and a husband that came home at nights. I had an underpaid job at the local supermarket checkout and a husband that, when he did come back at all, smelt of more booze than the local pub. She's got three lovely children, 'terribly well' accomplished in music and sport. I have one complete tramp of a teenage son, with foul language, body piercing and grade E in maths. He takes after his father. We couldn't have any more children. Perhaps it's as well.

Then there were the holidays. Sheila Johnson's family went for four weeks in the Caribbean every summer and other breaks throughout the year. I got a week in Ibiza with a drunken husband and a moronic son. They drive a Mercedes, and I've got a five year old Fiesta. I say 'got', but to be honest now I'm in here I haven't much idea what I've got. Some stuff had to be returned and Dave will probably have flogged the Fiesta to pay for more booze. When you think about it, who can blame me?

It all started last year. The Johnsons had gone to Cyprus; 'just for the week' were Sheila words, when she left me the list of things to do for them. It was only the usual stuff, water the plants, put the bin out, you know the kind of thing. We'd always been 'good neighbours' keeping keys for each other, but that list was the last straw. What was there to lose? The Mercedes wasn't doing anything while they were away, so I borrowed it. I hardly used any petrol and I left it exactly as I'd found it. Who was to know?

There was no problem from using the car, so the next time they went away I used it again and took advantage of a wider choice of clothing. I was bored with wearing jeans and the feel of pure silk against the skin is just irresistible. I put the dresses back after I'd used them. It wasn't as though I actually took anything. By the time of their main holiday last summer Johnny had joined in. He realised they had a better range of telly channels than we could afford, so he went round there to watch them. It was only later he installed the splitter and ran a cable across to our house, so he could get them any time.

It was fortunate that the electoral roll form came whilst they were away. I put myself down at that address. The Johnsons wouldn't check; no one does. None of the credit companies would extend further credit to me at my own address, with the county court judgements, but registering there meant I could set the credit cards up and then change the address later. I managed to get applications done for three cards and a loan for £10,000.

If I'd stopped there, I might have been able to explain things to the judge, but you know how it is. When you're bringing someone's post in for them, you notice the envelopes. It doesn't take much to steam one or two open to take a note of their car breakdown number and their credit card details. At the end of the day they weren't going to notice one or two small additional amounts amongst the large number of items already on their credit card statements. When you arrange items to be delivered to the 'credit card holder's address' no one gets suspicious. All I had to do was be the 'helpful neighbour' taking in their delivery whilst they were away. I was surprised that questions weren't being asked. I got through Christmas OK; it was great being able to buy my friends some decent presents for a change. Then, early in the new-year, I was fed up with being able to use a decent car occasionally, I wanted one for every day. I started to work out when to complete the paperwork, to clear it all whilst they were in the Canaries at Easter. It was important to find a car that was available immediately, to get the timing just right. It meant I had to have the model without tinted glass but I got the full satellite navigation system and electric heated seats. I'd noticed that there were quite a lot of transactions going through their savings accounts for £5,000 and £10,000 at a time, both coming in and going out, so I reckoned that if I set the repayments up as similar amounts, the Johnsons wouldn't notice.

I took delivery of my beautiful BMW just before they came back. I parked it proudly in the driveway. My friends thought that Dave must have come good at last and that I was going up in the world. Life was great. I took the girls out and felt so proud. The next thing I needed was a decent holiday. I thought I'd go on a cruise, just me, no Dave or Johnny.

It was whilst I was away that the problems started, not with next door exactly. To be honest, I think they were still none the wiser.

"Mr Cole, I'm Detective Inspector Hunt. Could you tell me whether you are the owner of a blue BMW registration number RE07MDF?" That's what Dave said the bloke said, although he was drunk at the time, Dave that is not the detective. Well Dave said it was his wife's and that I was away on holiday. Detective Inspector Hunt said he was looking forward to talking to me when I returned from 'my little trip'. The detective was looking forward to it so much that he met my plane at Heathrow and invited me to go for a chat. I don't think it was optional, not from the handcuffs he held out for me.

"Mrs Sylvia Cole, I am arresting you on suspicion of money-laundering. Anything you say..." You know the drill. There may be a lot of things I am guilty of, but money-laundering is not one of them. To be quite honest, I don't know what it is exactly. I was so far out of my depth I would have needed scuba diving equipment to touch the bottom. When I got to the Police Station, I asked for a lawyer, but asked if it could be a cheap one as I'd overspent on the cruise.

My lawyer seemed to think I was in more trouble than you might have thought from my neighbours going to the police, after discovering the things I'd 'borrowed'. The police wouldn't tell us what was going on, not at that stage anyway.

My lawyer made me tell her the whole story before letting me say anything in the police interview room. It was strange because they kept asking whether I knew where the money had come from, that went into the Johnson's savings account. I said I presumed they'd earned it, but the police didn't seem satisfied with that.

I passed Steve Johnson in the corridor at the Police Station as I was taken back to my cell. It was strange him being in handcuffs too, when he was the person I'd borrowed things from.

Eventually we found that it wasn't next door that had gone to the police at all. As it turned out, the Johnsons were aware of one or two of the things I'd borrowed, but didn't want to make a fuss. I thought that was very decent of them, all things considered. I was caught as part of a bigger investigation into drug smuggling and money-laundering. It turns out that Mr and Mrs Johnson's holidays in the Caribbean were to visit their key 'sources' and keep them 'sweet'. The police were looking at all the amounts going into and out of their accounts as part of a money-laundering investigation and my BMW got caught up in the process. It's been impounded now, so I'm back to just the Fiesta, or at least I would be if I could get out to use it.

After all the Johnsons had done, you wouldn't credit it. When Dave came to see me last week he brought me a cutting from the local paper. Although Steve Johnson was sent to prison for seven years, despite her involvement, Sheila only got a suspended sentence and here's me, not having done anything wrong and I'm in here for three years. On top of all our other problems, the Johnsons have stopped the extra telly channels coming through to our house and Mrs Johnson has taken her door key back. The cheek of it, you'd think she didn't trust us! Mind you, I wouldn't want crooks like them having my front door key anyway. You never know what they might do.

THE OLD OAK TREE

"Well it matters to me." Gavin stamped down the garden clutching his box of crayons with grim determination. "If you won't help me, I'll do it on my own." His little brown spaniel trotted faithfully behind.

'Don't get involved.' That's what Aunty Vi said, but he was already involved. If the Council chopped those trees down where would he get his conkers? Where would the squirrels get their acorns? Where would the birds live? Where would he ride his bike, other than the roads? Why didn't grown-ups understand what was important?

He made his way to the garden shed that doubled as his den, drew back the small black metal bolt, then put the box on the window ledge so that he could use both hands to tug open the door, which always stuck. Once it had finished creaking on its misshapen hinges he propped it open and went inside. He rolled out a large sheet of paper, which was slightly damp from being kept in the shed. Then opening the box, he took out the biggest, blackest felt pen he could find and started to draw on the paper.

He concentrated very hard to make the letters big enough and clear enough to read and he checked the spelling carefully as he wrote. Trees with two 'e's in it; he formed them as carefully as he could. He sat on the floor and wrapped his arms around Bruno. "You know it's important, don't you? I want trees not some car park. Where will you go for a walk if they take the trees away? We've got to stop them." Then he took some Blu-Tack out of the box and put it in his pocket, rolled up the poster and with that carefully in one hand and Bruno's lead in the other, he set off up the garden, ducking as he passed the kitchen window and headed along the road towards the copse.

It was the oak tree he loved most; seeing the squirrels chasing round its trunk was always fun. He tied Bruno to a post, rolled the Blu-Tack into sticky balls and then attached the poster to the trunk of the tree by its corners. He sat down with Bruno on the ground below the poster. He had no idea what to do next. All he could think was to sit and wait, though he wasn't quite sure what for.

He'd been there forty minutes, counting traffic and birds to pass the time, when he saw Grandpa walking towards him.

"Come on, lad, it's time to come home. Tea's nearly ready; your Mum's worried about you."

"Don't you think it's a beautiful tree, Grandpa?" He put his hand against the trunk of the oak, its gnarled bark rough against his palm.

"Yes of course I do. We didn't have bicycles when we were young, but we used to get conkers from the horse chestnuts here, just like you. I don't remember the grey squirrels, but there were certainly birds nesting."

"Grandpa," he said, slipping his small hand into the weathered palm of the old man. "Didn't you say you fought in the war to make this a better world?"

"Well yes, but..."

"These trees are part of my better world. When I'm old, I want to stand here with my kids and tell them about the birds nesting here when I was young and how I rode my bike round the trees and across the mud. Dad just says 'you'll understand when you get older', but I think he's just not bothered. Well I am bothered and I want to save the trees."

The old man looked down at his grandson with tears in his eyes. "I'm proud of you, Gavin." He smiled. "D'you know, I think I can be bothered too. What do you think we need to do?"

"I dunno. When Mum wanted the school to put a new fence around the playground, all the mums wrote on a piece of paper and gave it to the school. D'you think if we get lots of people to write their names down the Council might listen to us?" Bruno trotted along beside Gavin as they made their way home.

"I don't know," Grandpa said. "It's not the Council that owns the land. It's some bigwig who doesn't live near here. He's probably just interested in the money. But we could certainly try a petition."

Gavin ate his tea with Grandpa and they worked out what the petition needed to say. Grandpa wrote it out. "We the undersigned would like the land by Washbrook Lane to remain as a copse and green area and not be turned into a car park."

"We must put 'please' on the end; Mum always says I should say please."

"Ok," said Grandpa smiling, "I'll add 'please'."

The following day was Wednesday and Gavin and Grandpa worked to get as many signatures on the petition as they could. Gavin asked all his friends, teachers and staff at school, Grandpa asked everyone at the bowls club and at the day centre he went to. After school, Grandpa was there to meet Gavin and they began to call at the houses they passed on the way home.

It was unusual for Gavin's family to sit down for a meal together in the evening. Gavin was always hungry when he came in from school and his father was often late home from work. Today Gavin and Grandpa didn't get in from collecting signatures until 6.30pm and Gavin's Dad came in soon after.

"What have you been doing today, Gavin?" Dad asked as they all tucked into spaghetti Bolognese.

Gavin passed the petition across to his father. "We've been getting names to save the trees. I need yours too."

Gavin's father dropped his fork with a clang on the side of his plate. He looked instantly red in the face, "I forbid my son to be involved in this," he stormed. "Gavin please go to your room." Gavin meekly left the table. He knew when not to confront his father and this was definitely one of those times. However, as soon as his back was turned he scowled and stuck out his tongue. He went and stood just outside the room and put his eye to the gap by the hinge to see what was happening.

Grandpa stood up, "And I forbid you, Tom, my own son to be such a jumped up, money grabbing leech, working for the developer. Now we're even. What difference does it make?"

"Tom, what does Grandpa mean, 'working for the developer'?" Gavin's Mum looked flustered.

"Nothing, darling," Tom dabbed his mouth with his serviette.

"Nothing!" Grandpa shouted. "I'll give you nothing. I'm ashamed to call you my son. Do you want to tell Jean or shall I?"

"It's just," Tom shifted awkwardly. "I'm doing the legal work for Frank Martin, the site developer."

"Don't let Gavin hear you say that."

"It's ok, Grandpa," said Gavin coming back in, "I was listening in the hall, I already heard." Then looking his father in the eye he said, "Please may I have his phone number? I'd like to talk to him."

"Don't be ridiculous. You're only eleven years old!"

"What difference does his age make, Tom? That isn't how we've brought him up." Jean looked sternly at her husband. "What harm can it do for him to speak to Mr Martin?"

"It won't make any difference. The scheme's too far advanced. There's too much money in it. He'll only cause us embarrassment. There's going to be a car park and that's that."

"Nothing's actually signed yet though, is it?" Grandpa rubbed his chin.

"Well, no. Not actually signed." Tom looked uncomfortable.

"But I still want to try. If I don't talk to him I'll never know if he might have said yes." Gavin held his father's gaze.

"Tom, he's come this far, we've got to let him try." Gavin's Mum put her hand on Dad's arm, "Please."

Tom looked beaten. "Ok. I have to see him in London tomorrow. I'll give him your petition?"

"No," Gavin chose his words carefully, "I'm sorry Dad, I don't trust you."

Tom he opened his mouth to respond but closed it again, and nodded slightly.

"Come on, Tom, did I bring you up so badly that you've forgotten the things that really matter? Mother would be ashamed of you." Grandpa looked his son in the eye and held his gaze. "Give the boy a chance, let him dream. Not everyone is as focussed on money as you are."

"Ok," Tom said to Gavin, "in that case you'd better come with me tomorrow."

"But, it's a school day, Tom."

"Don't worry, Mum, I promise I'll catch up." Gavin gave her a beaming grin. Then he threw his arms around his Grandpa's neck and said, "We're going to do it, Grandpa."

Gavin was ready early next morning. He dressed as smartly as he could and Grandpa rang to wish him luck before he set off. The train journey itself was quite exciting, although he'd been to London a number of times before, but never on a school day. He sat opposite Dad and watched the passing countryside out of the window. Dad sat and read the newspaper.

"What's he like?"

"Who?" Dad seemed to have almost forgotten that Gavin was there.

"Mr Martin. What's he like?" Gavin asked patiently, not wanting to blow his chance of seeing him by annoying his Dad first. This wasn't the time for smart replies.

"He's a very busy man," was all his father said.

They walked to the taxis in silence and were soon heading through the back streets of London to the offices of Frank Martin Associates. Gavin thought how boring this part of London looked compared to where he'd been before. It was all grey stone buildings and lots of traffic. He thought how sad it must be to have so few places to watch squirrels play.

Frank Martin's offices were on the 24th floor. The reception had a view across London unlike anything that Gavin had ever seen. He stood by the windows, transfixed, clutching the petition to his chest. His father asked him to wait whilst he explained to Mr Martin what was happening. Gavin was miles away, looking down at the twists of the river, with its many bridges criss-crossing the city. He didn't hear the heavy footsteps behind him. Then a voice said, "It looks like a giant jigsaw puzzle doesn't it?"

Gavin looked up into a kindly face, "I don't think I could do such a big jigsaw."

"No, I suppose not. I've got a grandson about your age. He calls me Pops. You can call me that too, if you'd like to. And what's your name?"

"I'm Gavin. I've come to see Mr Martin."

"And what do you need to see Mr Martin for?" The man asked, sitting on a stool near the window to be closer to Gavin's height.

"I've come about the trees."

"Which trees are those? There aren't many around here."

"No they aren't around here. They're near where I live. It's where I ride my bike and walk Bruno, my dog. Mr Martin wants to cut the trees down to build a car park, but we don't want a car park, we want trees." Then he paused before adding, "I get my conkers there too."

"Is that right? I played conkers against my grandson not long ago. He won of course. When I was a child, we kept the conkers until the following year to make them harder."

Gavin grinned from ear to ear. "We do that too."

"There were lots of trees when I was young," the man said wistfully. "We were never short of places to play in those days."

"It's the only place I can play safely in Triford. Mum says I need to be older before I can ride my bike on the road. Bruno can run about there safely too."

"Well I'd better be getting back to my meeting young man. It's been nice talking to you."

Gavin turned back to the window and was watching a boat moving slowly along the river when he heard Dad, "Gavin, you can come in now."

Gavin walked over to the big wooden doorway. "I'm

scared, Dad."

"You'll be fine." His father seemed softer with him. "Just say what you came to say, but don't be too disappointed when he says no."

"Ok."

Tom walked back into the room, "Frank, allow me to introduce my son Gavin."

Frank Martin came around from behind the desk grinning.

"Pops," said Gavin in surprise.

"Gavin, that isn't how you address Mr Martin."

"No, Tom, it's fine, we've already met," said Frank Martin. "Come and sit down and show me your petition."

Gavin sat beside him on the couch, whilst Dad continued to stand awkwardly just inside the door.

"Now why don't you tell me about the oak tree? Your Dad said that's your favourite."

"Yes, I love the feel of its bark and the shape of its leaves and watching the squirrels chase around it."

"D'you think you might like to show me, if I were to visit?"

"Oh, yes please," said Gavin. "You could meet Bruno too."

"Then why don't we do that? I'll get my secretary to sort something out with your Dad. In the meantime I'm going to think about what you've told me and then I'm going to write you a letter to tell you what I've decided. Will that be ok?"

"Yes, Pops," said Gavin, "thank you."

"Now, if we've finished, I'll get my chauffeur to bring the car to drive you back to the station, if that's all right?" Frank Martin looked across to Tom for approval. He gave an uncomfortable nod.

Gavin was full of excitement on his way home. "I like Pops, he's very nice. Do you really think he'll come to see us?"

"I don't know," said Dad, rather more sullen than his son.

Gavin didn't have long to wait for the letter. It was there when he arrived home from school the following day. It was addressed to him personally and marked 'private and confidential'. "What does that mean?" he asked when Grandpa handed him the letter.

"It means it's just for you."

Inside Gavin found a hand written note and an important looking letter on headed notepaper. The note said:

"Gavin,

I hope you like the letter. I'm looking forward to watching the squirrels with you and perhaps we can have a game of conkers too.

Best wishes

Pops"

Gavin took the letter. "You read it."

Grandpa proceeded to read aloud:

"To the Triford Council,

Dear Sirs,

Re: Washbrook Lane

I regret to inform you that the car park construction will not be going ahead. Instead I would like to designate the land as a conservation area for the people of Triford and I will be appointing my representative Gavin Tremlow to be in charge of all future decisions concerning this land.

I will make funds available to Master Tremlow for the development of a nature reserve and such other facilities

appropriate to the site, to benefit the people of Triford.
    Yours faithfully
    Frank Martin."

Grandpa looked at Gavin with tears streaming down his cheeks. "You did it, Gavin. You believed in something and you did it."

"No, Grandpa, we did it. You believed in me and we did it together. It was you, me and Dad. I couldn't have done it without him either."

"No I suppose you couldn't," said Granddad, chuckling to himself.

"Do you think Mr Martin fought in the war too?"

"I don't know, Gavin. There're lots of ways to fight for a better world. You just need to know which side to fight on."

A TEST OF FRIENDSHIP

"Do you have a better suggestion?" Annie poured another glass of Chardonnay and sat back on the settee. She angled the fluffy white teddy to wave his paw at her friend.

"You're bonkers. You could adopt." Karen shook her head in disbelief. "And telling me that Bear needs a pair of little arms to hold him is no justification. You could have left him in the store."

"It's all right for you. You have men queuing up, with your blonde hair and blue eyes. I've tried internet dating and where did that get me? And you know I can't walk past a Mothercare store without going in." Annie threw the newspaper down on the table. The page was folded so that the advert was uppermost.

"The only internet date that went really wrong was what's his name, the one who set fire to the menu in the restaurant!" Karen said, laughing.

"None of them were suitable. One thought he was in love with me after a week and what about Barry?" Annie smoothed the creases from her pencil skirt.

"Ok, so you've had your share of deranged blokes. You'd have been crazy to stay with Barry, but this is sheer madness." Karen held up the newspaper and patted the back of her hand against the advert. "At least you haven't published your phone number."

"You know how much I long to have children and my body clock is ticking."

"It would have to be about to strike midnight before you placed an ad like this." Karen read the advert again 'Wanted, one night of sex as sperm donor for single woman. No strings attached. No ongoing support required. Must be blood donor.'

"Why 'must be a blood donor'?"

"Because they'll have been tested for HIV."

"Have you thought this through, Annie?"

"What have I got to lose? I'll have blokes queuing up. I can choose the most suitable one."

"Your one night stand with Peter wasn't much use."

"Well how was I to know he'd insist on using a condom?"

"Aren't there any legal implications? If it was as easy as that for a man to walk away it would be happening all the time."

"It does! Besides, if I don't put his name down on the birth certificate who are they going to chase after?"

"But what happens if your 'no strings attached' man suddenly wants to play father and see his little kiddiwink?"

Annie went quiet.

"You'd not thought about that had you?"

"I suppose I thought it wouldn't happen. If he's not involved after the first night then he probably won't think about it. I suppose it could be useful to have him around from time to time."

"You're not looking for a sensitive type then?" Karen looked back at the advert with its border and bold type. "You didn't mean them to miss it, did you? And whose idea was it to put this in the motoring section?"

"I wanted men to see it. Not just the losers looking through the personal ads."

"Hello! Wakey, wakey. I've got a bunch of roses here for

you to smell. We are the losers looking through the personal ads What are you looking for?"

"I thought maybe, tall. Men are nothing if they're not at least 5'10" these days. Dark hair and maybe brown or blue eyes. Definitely not overweight. For a start I've got to have sex with him, so I don't want him to be too gross. No body odour and not too hairy. I'd like him to be solvent too and preferably not married. I do hate blokes that cheat."

"And how exactly are you going to find all this about him if you don't go out with him first?"

"I thought I could get them all to fill in a questionnaire."

"You're expecting a bloke to be prepared to go through all those questions just for a free night of passion, when they can go down to The Prince of Orange and pick up some tart any night of the week, no questions asked."

"I want to be able to tell the baby good things about their father."

"This will be a man you don't know, who you will have no photos of and you'll have this ad to show to the child for how they were conceived. When are you likely to ovulate anyway?"

"Next Tuesday."

"I'd better be going. I've got a date with Charlie. I'm thinking of dumping him. Shall I get him to apply?"

"What's wrong with him?"

"Well apart from the washing that I've already mentioned, he's just not my type. He thinks a night out is a trip to the kebab shop."

Maybe it was going to work out after all. She'd fancied Charlie right from when Karen started seeing him. Karen had told her a few of his bad habits, but she wasn't planning to live with him.

"See you later." Annie called as Karen headed to the

door.

A couple of hours later the doorbell rang. Annie was feeling a little tipsy, having finished off the rest of the bottle of wine. She sobered up quickly when she saw who was on the doorstep.

"Charlie!"

He shifted from leg to leg. "Sorry to bother you, Annie. Karen said I should come round. You might be able to cheer me up."

Annie gulped. It was one thing talking to some nameless bloke who had applied in response to an ad, but quite another thing explaining her desperate need for a baby to a man she knew.

"Er, come in."

He walked past her into the apartment and slumped into a chair. With his head in his hands he broke into heaving sobs. "Oh, Annie, I'm sorry. Karen's just dumped me. I should have gone straight home."

Annie was stunned by his sudden show of emotion. She almost felt cross with her friend for hurting him. She didn't know what to say and sat waiting for him to get through it. Concentrating on the thought that his socks may not have been washed for several days was certainly helping.

"Tea!" She said. "That's good at times like this. I'll put the kettle on."

She went through to the kitchen and left Charlie to pull himself together. She didn't feel in too much of a rush to go back. How on earth could she explain to him what it was that Karen had sent him round for? It almost seemed cruel to treat the whole relationship thing so lightly when he was obviously upset by what had just happened.

To her surprise, when she came back Charlie had recovered and was smiling wickedly at the paper he was reading. "Have you seen this?" He pointed to the ad. "Can you believe that there's actually a woman advertising for a one night stand? That would be just what I needed to get over Karen. She didn't deserve me anyway. Do you mind if I tear this out?"

Annie could feel herself blushing. "There's no easy way of saying this. You don't need to keep the paper. It was me that placed the advert."

Charlie spluttered on his tea. "You! But you don't need to pick blokes up like this. You're so, so... well fanciable I suppose."

"Thanks," she said grinning.

"Do you want to... you know?"

"Well I don't need to until Tuesday."

"But there'd be no harm in a bit of practice. I could even throw a kebab in afterwards."

Her friend's words came flooding back to her. "I don't think so thanks. I'll wait to see who applies. I think you'd better leave."

Charlie looked up sadly, "Not even a little romp to cheer me up?"

Annie smiled at him. "No Charlie, not even a little romp. I think these things only work when you don't know the other person. I'm sure you'll find a lovely girl and if you're desperate, you could try The Prince of Orange."

Once he was gone Annie went to check her email. There were three hundred and twenty-two replies. She began to read. They could be broken down into three categories, saddos, weirdos and potential. She put the religious zealots that said she was going to burn in hell under weirdos. Eventually, the possibles were down to twenty-six. She replied to each of them asking if they were free on Tuesday and could they send a photo.

One that seemed to be promising turned out from the photograph to be Barry, who was back to responding to the small ads. She wondered how he had got past the weirdo pile. It made her realise that they, like her, had not been using their real names. She wondered what would happen if she put down 'Roger Rabbit' on the birth certificate.

She arranged the meeting with Clint Eastwood at a small hotel on the edge of the town. She knew the protocol for dating someone off the internet, meet in a light place, let someone know where you are and let them know you are safe afterwards, but what was the protocol for unbridled passion with a stranger? She started to think of all the things that could go wrong. Why hadn't it crossed her mind that they might lie about being a blood donor? There was nothing else for it. She emailed Clint calling the whole thing off and then rang Charlie.

"Don't ask any questions. Come round right now and have sex with me. Oh and please don't mention kebabs."

"You're kidding, right?"

"No, not kidding. Just do it before I change my mind."

"Do I need to bring anything?"

"Nothing, just you!"

He arrived in under twenty minutes and they managed to barely look at each other as they undressed and went to bed. It was even more embarrassing when it was all over. She grabbed her clothes and went into the bathroom.

She was just doing up her jeans when the phone rang. It was Karen. She answered a little breathlessly.

"Annie, it's me. You're never going to believe this. It's a good job you didn't sleep with Charlie."

"Why?" Annie was aware her voice came out very high.

"I've just found out I'm pregnant. I'm thinking of getting back together with him. He is going to be the child's dad.

Oh! It's Tuesday isn't it. How's it going with Clint?"

"Fine. Just fine." She squeaked.

She hung up and went back to the bedroom where Charlie was snoring.

"Wake up. You'd better go. I think we should keep this whole episode to ourselves. No one ever needs to know that we did this."

"Why?" He asked sounding sleepy.

"Trust me. This is definitely a secret we both want to keep."

ON THE BEAT

"I am not getting on that thing." Dave scowled at the heavy-framed bicycle leaning against the wall of the police station. "I've driven a squad car for more years than I can remember. I am not getting on a bicycle." Admittedly the bicycle looked built to withstand the rigours of his bulky frame, but that wasn't the point.

"But it's the Guv'nor's instructions. He wants us 'closer to the community'. There are four of us. We all start tomorrow."

"Let the Guv'nor get closer to the community if he wants to, but I am not getting on that bicycle or any other." Dave stormed off, leaving more slightly built PC Steve Trent grinning.

Dave slammed the door as he entered the house.

"Hi, honey," Sylvia called from the top of the stairs, "It's a good job our house was built to withstand violent assaults."

Dave grunted. He went through to the kitchen and got a beer out of the fridge.

"Is this a bad day you want to talk about or one you want to brood on?" Sylvia asked as she joined him and began to prepare the vegetables for dinner.

"What hair-brained idea is that wretched Chief Constable going to come up with next?" Dave began to help with the cooking, pummelling the steak with a tenderiser. The steak didn't stand a chance. "Community policing indeed! What's wrong with policing the community from the inside of a car? That's what I want to know. No one expects to see a copper on the beat without suitable transport. You want someone who can get to an emergency quickly, someone who can arrive in five minutes, fresh and ready for action, not hot and sweaty and needing a rest."

"Do I take it he wants you walking the streets?"

"It's worse than that, love. He wants me on a bicycle. Me, Dave Jones, all six foot four of me, on a bicycle!"

"You've been saying you want to get fit."

"In private! I want to get fit in private, not in front of the yobs I'm trying to police. Maybe it's time to quit and do something else. Perhaps this is just the push I needed. I could take retirement and then find something else."

"Or... just maybe you'll enjoy it, if you try. After all, you are the one that says policing has moved too far away from where the real problems are." She kissed him on the cheek. He put his arms round her shapely figure.

"'Get the youngsters out on the beat', I said. I did my share of that when I joined the force all those years ago. You expect certain privileges as you get older and a bike is not a privilege. A decent car is a privilege. A desk you don't have to share is a privilege. A pigeon-hole you don't have to stoop down to is a privilege. Not a bike."

There was a fine drizzle as Dave pulled into the car park at the police station the following morning. Despite his blustering, he was prepared for the worst and it wasn't long before he found himself cycling down High Street and off towards the Cranfield Estate. That would be his 'pleasure' for the morning.

A lanky boy with a cigarette hanging from his mouth was tinkering with a motorbike. "Hey! PC Jones, someone nicked your motor?"

How he wanted to tell the little thug where to go, but instead he pulled up. "We're smart this morning. No work again, Tippett?"

"Nah, got laid off Thursday. It's the same everywhere. Your lot are going to be busy, way things are."

As Dave got back on his bike to carry on, he began to realise that despite the weather he wasn't feeling so bad and it certainly made it easier to speak to people. He noticed two youngsters over by the bins and cycled in their direction. They started to run off down the path and he was able to follow them on the parallel cycle track, catching up with them before they'd gone far.

"No school, Darren?"

"Leave it out. You're as bad as our mum," said the boy who looked no more than about twelve.

"And she'll be even worse when I get the Social Services to pay her a little visit because you're playing truant. If I hear you made it in late to classes I won't put a call in, this time. Now off you go, both of you." As he cycled off, he couldn't help thinking if he'd been in the car he wouldn't have been able to catch that pair. He smiled.

As he headed through the estate he saw an elderly lady trip with a large bag of shopping and within seconds he had cycled up to help. "You all right?"

"I'll just sit here a minute," she said as he started to gather up the groceries.

"Do you need an ambulance?"

"No, I'll be ok. I just need to get to the flats over there, if you could help me up."

He lifted her gently and then supporting the shopping on the handlebars, he walked the lady slowly towards the flats.

"It's a good job you were there. It is nice to see a friendly policeman around," she said, smiling up at him. "Would you like a cup of tea?"

"Thank you, but I'd best be getting off if you're sure you'll be all right now." He put the bag of shopping into the kitchen and went out through the front door, closing it behind him. He went down the single flight of urine scented stairs. It was no wonder that so many of the youngsters from this area got into trouble, when you saw how they lived.

He peddled back across the estate as the clouds began to part. It felt good to have the sun on his face, even if he was wearing thick protective clothing. He smiled, enjoying the breeze as he peddled a little faster. Just then the two brothers he'd seen earlier came out of the cul-de-sac to Dave's right. They were on their bicycles now.

As they joined him, Darren, a slightly overweight boy in sweatpants and a blue hoodie, shouted, "Race you to the top of Hunter's Lane," and with that he peddled off turning back to see if the policeman was following.

He needed to catch up with them for not being in school. He stood up on the pedals to get momentum and went chasing after them. For a moment Dave felt like a child again. He was just crossing the junction with Dickens Way when he hit a pothole and went over the handlebars of the bike, landing in a mangled heap with his bike in the middle of the road.

The next thing that PC Jones knew, he was waking up in hospital, his arm immobile in a sling. PC Steve Trent was standing next to his bed.

"Good to see you back in the world, Dave. How are you feeling?"

Dave paused for a moment, still dazed with concussion. "Rough."

"At least your arm is only sprained. If it makes you feel any better, while you were waiting for the ambulance someone nicked your bike."

"Who called the ambulance?"

"I don't know. Apparently it was an anonymous call from a mobile."

Darren Fairchild, thought Dave smiling as he remembered their race. He wondered what would go into the official report. He couldn't very well say that he was racing a couple of kids when he had his accident. Perhaps he could say that he was trying to apprehend a known criminal, after all, chances were that it was Darren and his brother who had stolen his bike.

It was two weeks before Dave was out and about again, but he was confined to light duties based at the station. It was his second day back at work when he got a call from the front desk to say he'd got some visitors. Dave went through to find Darren and his brother standing in reception with a clean shiny bike.

"We thought we'd do it up a bit for you, sir," said Mike, the younger of the two.

"The wheel was buckled where you hit the pothole, so we found another wheel off an old bike at home. The one we found was a bit rusty but it's cleaned up ok," said Darren proudly holding the bike out for Dave to take. "I guess we felt it was our fault and we wanted to do something to say sorry."

Dave smiled at the two of them. "Thank you. I'm not allowed to ride for another two weeks, but I'll be back on the bike after that. Maybe next time I'll beat you to the top of the lane." As he spoke, Dave realised that despite his original misgivings, he was rather looking forward to being back on the bike again. It certainly seemed to have brought out the best in Mike and Darren, which had to be a good thing.

He was whistling as he opened the front door of the house that evening. Sylvia met him in the hallway. He wrapped his arms round her and planted a big sloppy kiss on her cheek.

"Let's go out for dinner tonight. I'm starving."

"Do I take it that the Gov'nor has backed down from his latest idea?" She asked.

"Not exactly," Dave said. "Let's just say that I may have come round to his way of thinking."

THE GUIDES AUCTION

"Which part of 'no' did you not understand?" Dad loosened his tie, removed his jacket and threw it over the back of a chair. "All I want to do tonight is watch the football with a glass of beer and some peace and quiet."

"But, Daddy, you said you'd come. You promised." Madeleine twisted her body into a perfect pleading sculpture.

For once he wasn't buying that blue-eyed innocence that normally left him powerless in his daughter's hands. "But, nothing. I've had a long day and I don't want to go to the Girl Guides Charity Auction and that is an end of the matter."

"You run upstairs and get ready, Madeleine. I'll talk to Daddy."

"Ok, Mum." Her pigtails swung freely behind her head as she took the stairs at a run. She began singing to herself as she went.

"You know how much she's been looking forward to this, darling. You did promise you'd come. I know it's an England match tonight, but this has been in the diary for a long time." She sat on the arm of his chair and stroked the back of his neck. "And I do think they're planning to have a screen so that all you addicts can keep up with the score."

Dad started to relax at his wife's touch. It wasn't their fault he'd had a bad day and if the football was going to be on anyway, he might still have a good evening. He wondered if he could take his beer to the village hall with him. He sighed heavily. "Ok, I'll come, but don't expect me to buy anything."

His wife kissed him on his broad forehead. "We're going in fifteen minutes. There's a tea provided as part of the evening."

Dad forced a smile. "Just give me time to get changed into something more comfortable."

The hall was already filling up as they arrived. One of Madeleine's friends, neatly dressed in her guiding uniform, with identikit pigtails, handed them a catalogue on the way in.

"There are two parts to the auction," Madeleine said. "In the first bit no one else knows what you're bidding and the highest bid wins."

Mum began to read the catalogue. "The small items are all by closed bids and then the main items will be auctioned off after the meal. Why don't we go and have a look at what there is?"

Trestle tables topped with white table clothes were burdened with all sorts of oddities, ranging from bags of sweets to carefully labelled envelopes saying things like 'Spa Day' and 'Log Cabin Weekend'. Dad trailed behind the rest of the family, eyeing his watch for the start of the match.

"Oh, look, Daddy. There's a pink cover for an I-pod. Please can you buy that for me? Put a bid in for it, please, Daddy, please."

He smiled shaking his head at the ease with which his beautiful ten-year old could manipulate him. He knew she did it, but he enjoyed it, so where was the problem? "Ok, sweetie, but before you decide that's what you want, don't you need to look at everything else first?"

Her serious face was turned up towards his, "No,

Daddy. That's what I want. Lizzie has a cover on hers, but this is much nicer."

He looked at his watch. "I'm going in search of the TV, find me there when you need me."

Mum rolled her eyes. "Come on, Madeleine, let's sort out what we have to do."

Dad wasn't alone in wanting to watch the match and there was already quite a crowd forming around the television. He sat in an orange plastic bucket chair and made himself as comfortable as he could. He was just in time for kick off and was surprised to find that beer was available and that the guide leaders were providing an at-seat service.

The match was critical to qualification for the European Cup and it wasn't long before England had gone one nil down. Dad had almost forgotten that he was sitting in the village hall, although the chair was an aching reminder. Then approaching half-time, England was on the attack. It looked as though there might be a chance of scoring. There were not many Montenegrin players up with the action, when Madeleine came across to her father, holding out a piece of paper.

"Can you fill in my bid for the I-pod cover please, Daddy?"

"You do it, honey," he said, not wanting to take his eyes off the television screen.

"But, Daddy?"

"Not now, Madeleine. You fill it in. I just need to watch what's happening."

"How much shall I put?"

"I don't know. Six pounds fifty, six pounds seventy-five?" He jumped to his feet as England took a corner and missed the goal.

The football fans had their tea served to them at their seats during half-time, while they all argued about the quality of the referee and whether that early foul should have been a penalty. The atmosphere for the second half was charged and no one moved when it was announced that the main auction was about to start in the hall. By the seventy-third minute England had equalised and all the football fans were standing and shouting at the television. It was the eighty-seventh minute before they scored a second goal, which, as long as they held their lead for the final minutes of the game would give them qualification.

As soon as the match was over, Ben went off to find his family, a broad grin stretching across his face. The auction for the main items was coming to an interval and the results of the closed bids were about to be announced.

"Everything Ok? I don't suppose I've missed much. We won," he said as he slid into the chair next to Mum.

"I gathered that from the noise you all made and your beaming smile. Madeleine is ready to go up with the other Guides to give out the items auctioned." As Mum finished saying this, a group of girls trooped onto the stage carrying the items for the closed bids.

Dad sat smiling to himself, the warm glow of the football win carrying him through the tedium of the rest of the evening. He didn't care that Mrs White had paid fifteen pounds for a poinsettia or that Mr Digby had paid twelve pounds fifty for a garden gnome. He was letting it all wash over him until he heard his own name being called.

"Ladies and gentlemen, I'd like to ask our star for this part of the evening to come up to the stage so that we can thank him properly for his wonderful generosity to the Guides this evening. Of course Mr Fellows' daughter is always willing to help out and now we know where she gets these qualities from."

Dad felt dazed as Mum, looking surprised, elbowed him to go up to the front. The hall broke into applause and feeling embarrassed he made his way to the front.

The announcer indicated for the audience to be quiet as Ben stepped onto the stage. "Ladies and Gentlemen, Mr Fellows has made the very generous donation of seventy-five pounds to buy the I-pod cover for his daughter Madeleine. I presume it's for Madeleine, Mr Fellows, I wouldn't have thought that pink was your colour."

By this time it was hard for Ben to hear what was being said over the cheers from the crowd. He was sure that the lady had just said seventy-five pounds, but he must have misheard her. He looked across at Madeleine whose innocent face was beaming at him. The crowd wouldn't be cheering for six pounds fifty. He looked across to Mum who was on her feet applauding with the others. She looked so proud of him that he simply went and shook the announcers hand and accepted the I-pod cover that was being handed to him by one of the guides.

He went back to his seat still shocked by what had happened. "Ben you're amazing," said Mum. "And there was me thinking you were reluctant to support the Guides. What a lovely thing to do with your overtime from work."

He shook his head and although he opened his mouth to speak nothing came out. Just then he saw Madeleine standing at the side, putting the cover on the I-pod. He went over to her.

"What exactly did you write on the piece of paper, honey?"

"You said fifty or seventy-five and I didn't want to lose it, so I put seventy-five just like you said. Look, Daddy, isn't it beautiful."

Dad nodded, "Yes it's beautiful." He mussed her hair. He couldn't help thinking that it was probably hard to hear him over the din of the cheering. He only had himself to blame. It had been an expensive evening. He couldn't afford to do that often. It did feel good to be everybody's hero for once and at least England won.

He looked across at Madeleine proudly showing the cover to Lizzie and smiled to himself. She was oblivious to the mistake. Perhaps it was best to leave it like that for now.

MUSIC SAVED MY SOUL

Tom handed Tina the envelope of tatty notes and coins. "You can count it, £75, it's all there." He was delighted to be repaying every penny.

"It's ok. I don't need to, thank you." Tina smiled as she put the envelope in the pocket of her apron.

Tom knew she didn't want the money back, she made it a loan to save his pride and he was proud. He would never have accepted it if she'd given it to him.

"You must be as good as I thought, to earn it so quickly."

"I don't know about that. I just do my best. It feels good after all this time to be earning some money. I've got a room of my own now. It's not much, but it's a start." Tom shifted on the plastic chair. He had spent a lot of time sitting in this café area.

Tina was usually the other side of the counter, serving, but she had spent many of her own tea breaks sitting talking to him. "Does that mean you won't be coming here for meals anymore?" He saw the glistening of a tear in her eye.

The hostel had been a regular haunt for him after his roughest days on the streets, talking to Tina had been his path to recovery.

They were sitting either side of the same coffee table they had sat at a few weeks earlier.

"I can't do it. I'm not good enough. And besides, where am I going to get the money for a guitar?" Tom had slammed the leaflet down on the table, which rocked on its uneven legs.

Tina had picked up the leaflet and put it into the corner of his bag. Then she put her hand on his arm. "You can do it, Tom. You are good enough. I've heard you sing. You have a beautiful voice and you said yourself you used to play in a band. Trust me, you just need more confidence."

He pulled at the torn sleeve of his jumper and scowled. "Aren't you rather overlooking the fact that I'm down and out and I'm broke?" Damn her for having faith in him. No one was meant to get this close again. He picked up his holdall and headed out of the hostel, slamming the door behind him. The open air would do for the night, even if he could have had a bunk indoors.

The arch of the bridge was already taken, so he slumped down in a doorway and huddled under his grubby, moth eaten blanket. How had his life come to this? One minute he was happily married, with a beautiful wife, a home and a good job selling life insurance and the next he'd lost it all. He still found it hard to believe how it had happened. Sally had been far too young to die. He loved her so much and when she'd gone his world ended. After that the drinking had been the final straw. He couldn't let himself fall in love again. Not with Tina, not with anyone.

He had no idea why he thought moving to London would make any difference; maybe he was attracted by the anonymity. There is nothing as impersonal as a park bench and a blanket, washing in a fountain and scavenging for scraps.

He took out the leaflet and read it by the light of the streetlamp. The official Underground busking scheme did seem to be a good idea. If the stories were to be believed there were musicians making a reasonable living out of their pitch. Tom wanted so much to get back on his feet. He didn't want to spend the rest of his life on the streets. He pictured the softness of Tina's face and relived the sensation of her slender hand resting on his. He wondered whether she was always as kind to the people passing through the hostel. He wanted to do this for her, but he was terrified of where his feelings were taking him. He pulled himself up. More importantly he wanted to do it for him. He needed this. It couldn't do any harm to apply.

Despite his doubts, Tom trudged the streets in the fine drizzle looking in second hand shops for a guitar. Around lunchtime he started heading toward the hostel as he had done most days since he found it after five hungry weeks on the streets. He didn't fancy the day without Tina's smile, despite his cross words of the previous day. He saw his reflection in a shop window as he passed. Six months on the streets had taken their toll. He looked much older than his 28 years, though his thick brown curly hair helped to redress the balance. Then his eyes focussed on what was behind the glass and his mouth fell open. To Tom it was the most beautiful guitar in the world, but the price tag said £75. He drew his hand out of his pocket and shuffled the loose cents and pennies around his palm. He bit his lip. His shoulders stooped as he walked on towards the hostel.

He didn't look at Tina as she poured his tea. He took it to the table, which rocked as he leant on it. He put the busking leaflet under the wonky leg to keep the table firm and sat stirring the spoon round in the cup. He wanted to apologise to Tina, but didn't know where to start. He wanted to see her smile. What right had he to make anyone smile? He suddenly felt ashamed of his appearance and wanted to run away, but he'd done that once and there was nowhere left to run.

He was still stirring the tea when Tina came and sat the other side of the table. "Penny for them."

He shrugged.

"I thought we were friends."

He could hear the sadness in her voice.

Tom could feel tears in his eyes and brushed them away with his sleeve. "You're right," he mumbled. "I want to change my life, but I can't make a start." Then before he knew it he was telling her about the guitar he'd just seen. He sighed. "I mess everything up. I'm sorry."

He looked up into her angelic face. Despite his fear he wanted to kiss her. He wanted to hold her, but who would want to be kissed by an unkempt man in dirty rags. Most people crossed the street to avoid him.

She smiled at him and his heart grew wings. He couldn't let himself feel this way.

Tina slid the leaflet out from under the table leg and took a pen from her pocket. She passed them to Tom. "Just fill it in. You have to try. We can worry about the guitar if you get an interview."

She was right. He knew she was. "Where can I put as my address? They don't deliver mail to a bench."

"Put here. It's fine. The others use it. I'd better get back behind the counter. Will you be ok?"

He smiled at her and nodded. Then took the pen and began to fill in the form.

The following week, Tina handed him a letter. "Go on, open it."

"No, you do it for me. I can't." Tom's hands were shaking as he handed the envelope back to her.

Tina tore it open. "You've got an interview," she shouted dancing up and down and then throwing her arms round his neck and kissing him on the cheek. "I knew you could do it."

His shoulders slumped. "But I don't have a guitar and the one in the shop's gone."

"Stay there." Tina danced off to the kitchen.

He looked up to see her coming back carrying a guitar shaped package.

"Tina!" He ran towards her and lifted her into the air.

"Mind the guitar." She laughed.

"But, the money." He put her down and looked serious.

"I used my savings. It was only sitting in the bank doing nothing. You can pay me back from what you earn."

Tom opened his mouth, but no words came out. How could she believe in a homeless alcoholic? He sat up straighter. He would repay her, every single penny.

"What are you going to sing?" Tina straightened the tie they found with some other clothes in the donations box.

"The streets of London, Summer of 69 and Yellow submarine, to give a bit of variety."

"Knock 'em dead."

That had been a few weeks ago. Tom returned from his reverie and saw Tina looking shyly at him. "I don't suppose I'm entitled to meals here anymore. I've got to make my own way in the world now."

Tina looked disappointed. "I suppose I can always come and hear you play."

Tom fiddled with his cuff. He didn't want these times talking to Tina to stop, but he was frightened to risk getting hurt again.

"I'm there five days a week between 10am and 4pm. There isn't much point being there for rush hour, most people are in too much of a hurry to listen."

He suddenly realised how much he'd miss her when he moved on. Those beautiful bright eyes, the mousy hair even her thick-rimmed glasses looked amazing to Tom.

"I haven't told you the best bit yet." Tom longed to gaze into those eyes. "One of the other buskers asked if I would try out for the band he's in. I went on Tuesday; they practice in an old warehouse the other side of the river. They want me to join. The band is made up entirely of official buskers and has been together about eight months. Their old guitarist got a full time job so he had to quit the band. They've got a number of paid bookings coming up; it'll give me a regular income of sorts." He paused, twisting his sleeve. "Do you think you might like to meet me for a coffee sometime?" He heard his voice, but didn't feel as though it was him saying the words.

Tina looked up at him, beaming. "I thought you'd never ask. If you're sure, I'd love to."

THE QUEEN BITES BACK

"It's all very well that we step-mothers get a bad name," said Ariadne, fluttering her eyelashes and swishing her raven black hair into place. "A doe-eyed child cries foul and their dear daddy believes them. Well things are never as simple as they seem and Snow White wasn't the perfect little miss that she's made out to be. Oh, she could act the part when it came to visitors, but living with her was an altogether different matter." Her eyelids descended slowly as a look of sadness fluttered across her face.

Tom wanted to wrap his arm around her, but knew how unprofessional that would be, particularly with her being the Queen. Despite his years in tabloid journalism, he struggled to think of a clear sentence. He coughed slightly. His job was to write a positive piece about the Queen and as she crossed her long slender legs allowing her slit skirt to fall open, he couldn't help but think from where he was sitting that was going to be fairly easy.

"And what were the circumstances in which you started living with Snow White?"

He knew she didn't want to be doing this interview, but her publicity manager had told her it would be worth it to set the record straight. From what the other papers were saying, she could certainly do with someone on her side for a change.

"Well, it was tragic that her mother died when she was a baby. That's no start in life for any child. Then her father and I fell in love soon afterwards. I always knew that bringing her up was part of the deal. I didn't shy away from the challenge, or send her off to boarding school." She flashed Tom a brilliant smile.

He jotted on his pad, forewent own success. He could feel his heart pounding every time he looked at her. "Where was her father in all this?"

"He was busy being king. There was no way he could give up what he did to bring up little Snow White, so out of the goodness of my heart I gave up my career, modelling and moved into the palace to raise her up as best I knew how."

He scribbled model and added a smiley face after it. "I'm reluctant to ask, ma'am, but given how considerate you were, how did it all go so wrong?"

Ariadne swept the back of her hand across her forehead. "I know everyone thinks it was down to vanity, all because of some silly looking glass. Someone said it could speak and everyone believed them, but that was just a myth. Of course, I did have a mirror on the wall, but do you really think I spent my days talking to it? The truth was very different. I'd had seven years of Snow White's little temper tantrums. The pouts, the tears, the 'I want a new Barbie doll. Daddy would let me have a new Barbie Doll.' Then there was the 'You can't tell me what to do, you're not my mother.' Oh how that hurt. And the 'I'll tell Daddy,' when all I was doing was offering the smallest piece of advice on her behaviour."

"How did that make you feel?" Tom smiled in encouragement.

"There were so many times she told her Dad she loved him, but didn't have a word of thanks for me who had given up so much for her. But I took it all. I coped when she said she hated me. I coped with the goading and the wrapping her Dad round her little finger. I coped when she engineered fights between her Dad and me."

Tom could see a tear forming in the corner of her eye. She allowed it to slowly trickle down her cheek leaving a track of diluted mascara behind. He quickly passed her his clean white handkerchief and was thankful he'd got it with him. "When did you stop being able to cope?"

The queen dabbed her eyes with the handkerchief and smiled softly. "Thank you." She paused to blow her nose, rather more loudly than Tom was expecting from one so dainty.

"There are always straws that break the camel's back. It was when her father and I found we couldn't have children of our own. I was devastated, but there wasn't any support for me. No one understood the pain of having to bring up Snow White, looking at her every day, knowing she wasn't mine. Knowing that at the first opportunity she would turn me out of my own palace and cast me from her kingdom, a mere nothing despite all I'd done."

"How did that make you feel?" He leant forwards in his chair listening intently. He'd made far fewer notes than usual.

The tears started again and she looked down.

"I suppose you could say I had a breakdown, a moment of madness, but then I suppose there are many women out there who will relate to how I felt. Every day I looked at her and saw the child I couldn't have; the child that should have called me 'Mum' and loved me all her life long. I reached breaking point. It wouldn't be so bad if the other papers had dealt with me fairly, but oh no, they have to immortalise the idea that I was rotten to the core, if you'll pardon the pun."

Tom saw a flash of anger in her eyes and for a moment

wondered if he was forming the wrong opinion of this poor dear lady. It was clear she hadn't finished talking so he said nothing, but turned over a new page of his pad and wrote 'enigma'.

"I do admit that I got the huntsman to take her into the wood, but I never meant for him to kill her. 'Teach her a bit of a lesson,' I said. I might have said to lose her and let her find her own way back, but I never said 'kill her'. What kind of person do you think I am? The whole thing about asking for her heart to be removed and then cooked is just a legend." She swallowed hard and sat up a little, looking at Tom with eyes made large by her now smudged eye-liner. "I've always been partial to venison; it was only natural that the huntsman should bring a deer for me on his way back. When I think about it, I suppose she had to lay the story on thickly to get those poor gullible dwarfs to take her in. If she'd told them the truth, they'd never have given her house room.

I'll grant that she seems to have turned over a new leaf when she was with them and wasn't as bone idle as she was at home, but she was still the same basic vengeful little princess that I'd cared for. She'd been used to living in luxury, everything done for her. How she coped with seven little men burping, farting and leaving their dirty pots around the house is beyond even my comprehension. I have to give her credit where it's due, it would have been stressful for anyone serving supper for eight people every day, darning their socks and can you imagine how much washing they must have created, if they changed their clothes at all."

"Have you found this out by talking to Snow White since then?" Tom rubbed the pencil along his furrowed brow.

"Good heavens, no! I disguised myself to visit her, but it was only to check she was safe and well. With all that to contend with, it's no more than any loving step-mother would do. The first time, when I went as a peddler, I took some beautiful lace. How was I to know she couldn't cope with it being tied that tightly round her neck? She was all right when I left her; it was just unfortunate that she collapsed later."

Tom stopped smiling. "Was that the only time you visited her?"

"I went back dressed as an old woman and lovingly brushed her hair, it was simply a gesture of affection. I've no idea where the comb had picked up the poison. I can only think there must have been some lying around in the dwarfs' house. Perhaps they'd got fed up with her themselves."

Tom ran his finger round his collar and swallowed hard. "Was that the last time you saw her?"

The queen looked down. "When I went the third time I took her a beautifully ripe apple. I don't know how the whole poison story came about. I proved there was nothing wrong with it by eating some myself. I can only think that her appalling cooking had given her food poisoning. She'd never so much as cooked salad when she was in the palace."

Tom bit the end of his pencil and started to jot some of his thoughts. 'Is she what she seems?' 'Has anyone covered Snow White's version of events?' He spoke hesitantly. "I believe she recovered from that unfortunate episode."

Ariadne got up from the couch and was starting to pace the room making Tom feel nervous.

"What kind of friends did the dwarfs turn out to be? There she was, left in a glass coffin in the middle of the wood. They didn't even give her a decent burial. If it hadn't been for that Prince Charming she would have been left to decay in full view of everyone. Instead of which, one deftly applied Heimlich manoeuvre and she's back on her feet, thinking he's the most wonderful person in the world, but I'm sure he's not all he's portrayed to be. I'm surprised he looked at her twice after she'd been living with seven men at the same time. I mean, I don't like to cast aspersions, but who knows how low their morality had sunk. Can you really imagine that all seven of them had managed to resist her charms? Is it any wonder that one of them was called Happy?"

Tom looked at her beautiful face, but this time he saw her looking down her aquiline nose at him. He felt uncomfortable as she walked behind where he was sitting.

A steely determination had entered her voice. "Now here I am, accused of crimes of which I am clearly innocent, while little miss glad-rags is off marrying her Prince Charming. They say there's DNA evidence linking me to the crime of attempted murder, but how can it be my fault that she swallowed too large a lump of apple and was choking. My lawyer says I should plead guilty based on temporary insanity, but I'm innocent I tell you." Her nostrils flared as she spoke.

Tom moved further away from her outstretched hands.

"As always, she's got everyone on her side, twisting the story to serve her needs. Where's the gratitude for everything I gave up? And where's the king when I need him? So much for telling me he loved me. When it came down to it, he always did take his daughter's side rather than mine. He was so pleased to have her home. He wouldn't hear a word said against her."

"I think I've probably got all I need," said Tom, starting to gather up his things.

Ariadne turned to him with a flash of menace in her eyes. "I don't think you're going just yet." She hissed. "Even without the public support, I can still make sure she doesn't marry Prince Charming. You just wait until they get to the bit, 'Does anyone know of any lawful impediment...' Wait until the crowd holds its breath, desperate for the vicar to move on to the next bit. That's when I'll produce the evidence of Prince Charming's bigamy. He can't marry our darling little Snow White. He's already married to Cinderella. Now there's a news story for your front page!"

CHANGING PLACES

"I haven't even asked you yet what you're doing for the 'ols?" Lizzie grinned at her friend as the conveyor belt between them slowed to a stop.

"I'm off to Lanzarote tonight, just self-catering, mind," shouted Dora, pushing her overall into her bag. "What about you?"

"Let's just say I'm 'oping to pick up a good last minute deal," Lizzie replied, removing her hairnet from her greying brown hair. She'd been saving as hard as she could, but there was very little she could do with the sort of money she'd put by. She had thought of staying at home and using the money to decorate the lounge, it certainly needed it. That was until she'd seen that 'Changing Places' programme on the telly last week. Then she'd hit on an idea and knew exactly what she was going to do for the next two weeks. Never mind the house, Lizzie Smythe was going to change places.

The only thing she still needed to buy, to put her plan into action, was the wide brimmed hat with the oversized daisies on. It would do a good job of covering her tired face, with the crab-like wrinkles scuttling round her eyes and the broken veins streaking her pallid cheeks. When she tried it on, she couldn't help but think it made her look rather classy.

The factory clock said 4.15pm; there was still time to get to the Oxfam shop before it closed. Lizzie was grateful that they finished early for holiday fortnight; it would be good to be able to start her plan from first thing the following day.

Saturday was a fine bright morning as Lizzie checked that everything was ready. She looked in the mirror at the effect of her understated lipstick and blue-grey eye-shadow, bringing out the best in her still youthful eyes and laughed as she remembered Bert saying that she could scrub up all right when she put her mind to it. She checked her handbag one final time, picked up her sunglasses and newly purchased hat and went to catch the bus. She got off one stop short of the Mercedes garage, thinking it would look better to arrive on foot. She had chosen reasonably sensible heels to make getting about easier, although the sharp line of the jacket and narrow skirt were not the easiest things she'd walked in.

It was just before 10.00am as she approached the reception desk, held out her gloved hand and in the voice she'd been practising said "Darling, you should have a car for me to test drive."

The assistant simply looked at her hand, declining to shake it and said "What name is it?"

Lizzie handed him one of her crisp new business cards, which read 'Mrs Elizabeth Worthington-Smythe, Managing Director, Pendleton Hall, Salford Lane, Billingbrook.' Pendleton Hall had been a little joke between her and her ex-husband when they moved into their former council house. Fortunately, Salford Lane was a long road with a wide range of housing, leaving no one to suspect exactly which house it referred to. It sounded so much better than 'number 6' and as for the 'Managing Director', well she was the one that ran the house these days. The only real addition had been 'Worthington', she felt a double-barrelled name would fit the image she needed rather better than just plain 'Smythe'.

"May I see your driving licence?"

Lizzie was glad she hadn't gone for a completely fictitious name; at least it meant that all her real documents could be used. "I leave the 'Worthington' off official papers. I do rather find it gets in the way." She said in the same clipped tone as before.

"And if I could just take a few details of the model you are interested in," the young assistant continued.

Lizzie was already starting to enjoy her holiday as she told the gentleman that she would of course be paying cash and would want the top of the range convertible, with all the trimmings, but she quite understood if they didn't have one of those available for her to test today.

After twenty minutes she was on the road in a dark navy Mercedes, which for the next three hours was hers to enjoy. She placed the hat on the passenger seat and headed for her next appointment.

Pulling into the sweeping gravel drive, Lizzie found the estate agent already waiting for her. Awkward as it was, she donned the wide brimmed hat before leaving the car and as elegantly as possible, stepped out in front of the double oak doors.

She'd always wanted to look round Billingbrook Hall, where her grandmother had been a scullery maid, all those years ago. When she found that its current owners, Sir Geoffrey and Lady Penelope Tomlinson, had put the Hall up for sale she was overjoyed by the happy coincidence.

"Mrs Worthington-Smythe, Good Morning," simpered the estate agent as he led her through into the main hallway. He collected the post off the mat and put it on the growing pile on the circular table in the middle of the hall.

He didn't look at any of the letters or make to put them in his briefcase. Lizzie let out a relieved sigh.

"I'll show you around and then maybe you would like to have a look on your own."

Lizzie thoroughly enjoyed seeing the splendour of the Hall. She remembered to ask all her pre-prepared questions, playing her part to perfection. "How many staff is there accommodation for?" "Do you have details of where the marble came from, so that I can have it matched in any improvements I do?" It was amazing what you could pick up from watching one or two things on the telly.

As soon as she was free to roam, Lizzie made her way back to the pile of post and picked out three items addressed in her name. She had used the address to avoid showing up as a credit risk on a database search and she'd known from the local paper that the current owners of the house had recently gone abroad for six months.

She continued to have a look around before going back to the waiting estate agent and saying "Thank you. Yes, I like what I see, you'll be hearing from my lawyers." How good it all sounded. She smiled to herself as she went out to the waiting Mercedes.

With the car returned, Lizzie headed home to open her post.

"Dear Madam,

We are delighted to invite you and your husband for a free trial of our Luxury Forest Lodges. We will provide three nights free accommodation in one of our top of the range properties and all we ask is that you and your husband attend one of our sales presentations on the second day..."

Drat, she needed a husband. She hadn't thought about how

she was going to get around that one. She'd just tell them he'd been called away on important business. Maybe she would also hint that it was all very confidential. They'd be impressed by that. She also needed to arrange transport to get there. With everything else going so well she was sure she could resolve those minor technicalities, so she rang the number to make a booking. They could fit her in from Wednesday. She checked her schedule and decided she could rearrange her Porsche test drive to another day.

The second letter confirmed her appointment with the personal shopper in Harrods of Knightsbridge on Monday at 2pm. She'd used the tokens, so carefully collected from the papers left in the rest-room at work, to book her free rail trip in anticipation of the appointment. Now all she had to do was arrange for someone to call her away to an emergency at around 3.45pm, before there was any question of her paying for all the clothes she would have selected.

The third letter confirmed her appointment to be shown over a luxury yacht, which was for sale in a marina on the coast not far from Blackpool. Lizzie booked the bus from Billingbrook to get there on Tuesday the following week.

She looked at her diary. That left the BMW garage this Tuesday, Horse Racing a week on Thursday, where she planned to join in one of the hospitality tents and the Porsche test drive to rearrange. She sat and thought about whether there was anything else she wanted to fit in.

By the time Lizzie arrived at the Porsche garage the following week, the novelty of all the borrowed luxury was wearing thin. She wondered if Dora was having fun lying on a beach. Lizzie missed having some company and was even looking forward to going back to work.

"I'm sorry Mrs Worthington-Smythe," said the garage

receptionist, "we seem to have double-booked the car for the test drive."

If nothing else, Lizzie thought, an argument would spice things up a bit. "DOUBLE-BOOKED! What do you mean double-booked? I had my secretary confirm it with you only yesterday."

"Yes," said the receptionist. "I can understand your annoyance, but one of my colleagues has scheduled a drive for Mrs Harris-Jones. That's the lady waiting over there."

"Well it's my test drive." Lizzie started to get carried away. "I was planning to pay cash for a car straight afterwards, if I was happy with the drive."

"Perhaps you could each take the car for half an hour," suggested the worried receptionist.

"I shall go over there now and speak to Mrs Harris-Jones myself. I'm sure she will see sense."

Lizzie marched across the showroom towards the lady standing by the coffee machine. The receptionist scurried after her. "No, wait, please."

As the woman by the coffee turned round to see what the commotion was, Lizzie stopped in her tracks. "Dora! What on earth are you doing here?"

"I could very well ask you the same question Lizzie Smythe."

"But I thought you were in Lanzarote."

"And I thought you were going away on a cheap last minute deal."

The receptionist stood open-mouthed, looking at first one woman and then the other. "Do you two know each other?"

"I should say so," said Lizzie, suddenly smiling. "There won't be a problem with the test drive. We'll take the car out at the same time. Come on girl, let's go and have some fun."

Looking more perplexed than ever, the receptionist handed them the keys. The two women headed out of the showroom arm in arm.

"I don't suppose there's any need for me to ask how you've spent your holiday then," said Dora, grinning at her workmate.

"It's been fun, but it would have been far better if we'd done it together. Do you want to drive or shall I?" said Lizzie, dangling the keys in front of Dora.

PARIS

'Time to build her career,' her parents said. 'You can't be a waitress all your life.' That's what her parents thought, but Jenny really couldn't see why not. She'd at least enjoyed waitressing. As for this...

"If you're away from your desk or can't take a call, don't forget to sign out of your phone. And what are the circumstances in which you can be away from your desk?"

Jenny hated these little pep talks from Mr Clarke every week at the sales meeting.

"Death and authorised holiday." Craig rolled his eyes.

"That's right, Craig. Now team it's almost 8 o'clock. Remember your December targets and there's a weekend in Paris for the one who sells the most. Now, go team."

Jenny smoothed down her tight-fitting skirt and rearranged her ample bosom. There was no more putting off the inevitable. She wheeled her chair back around to her terminal and picked up the headset. She detested this job. She was applying for other things, but in the meantime this was her pay packet.

No matter how hard she saved she was never going to be able to afford a holiday to visit Philippe, the dark haired, chestnut eyed Parisian she'd met while waitressing last summer and thought about ever since. She shivered as she thought of his French accent making English sound so seductive.

She wanted that prize more than any of the others, but

however much she wanted it, she couldn't reconcile her longing with what she actually had to do to beat the targets.

You were always expected to sell more advertising space to the clients than they'd asked for. Just imagine what the checkouts in Tesco's would be like if they did that. 'Are you sure you only want six doughnuts? If you buy twelve and this nice long life bag, to add to the pile you've left in the boot of the car, you can have them all for a special package price.' No she couldn't see it. She logged into her terminal. Then there was the fact that she always got the crank calls.

"Southingham Express, how may I help you?"

"I don't know what I need to do. I've never done this before. My Arthur died last week."

"Would you like to place a notice of the death?" Jenny groaned. There were so few opportunities to really sell up on a death notice, except when you got relatives to outdo each other and put in ever more grotesque sugar sweet poems of remembrance.

"Oh no, it's nothing like that. The undertaker said he'd sort that out."

"Then how may I help you?" She sighed quietly. She could see it was going to be one of those days, every widow wanting to tell her their life story.

"I want to sell his things and I want to put a notice in the personals, find me a younger version."

Here we go again. Crank.

There was a giggle from the other end of the phone. "It'll need to be anonymous. I wouldn't want people to think it was in bad taste."

Jenny smiled, now here was an opportunity to sell some space. She took all the details, encouraging Mrs Jeffries to have borders and bold letters, an extra line here and there.

Yes, of course this was a good way to be spending her inheritance and if all went well it should bring in some more money from the fishing rod and garden shed. She glanced up at the board, which was flashing five calls waiting. If she could just speed Mrs Jeffries along, she might pick one of them up with no down time. Perhaps there was hope of that trip to Paris after all. If she could stand the pressure of working in this environment.

"Southingham Express, how may I help you?"

"There's a bomb."

Oh no, Jenny, remember your training. Call the supervisor into the call, keep them talking for as long as possible. They may be a crank, but they may be for real. These calls usually went through to switchboard, but they'd all been trained. It was one of the penalties of working at the newspaper. She pressed the alarm button and waved her arm in the air to attract the supervisor's attention.

Her voice was shaky as she said, "Please will you give me details of where it is?"

"It's in the post box on the corner of East Street. It's timed to go off at 9 o'clock."

"And who is this calling?" But the dial tone came back. The caller had hung up. She logged out of her headset and ran over to the supervisor.

"Did you get that Maureen?" Maureen was already dialling the police to alert them.

As Jenny stood there the boss walked past, "Death or authorised holiday, Jenny?"

"Neither Mr Clarke, I just had a . . ."

"Then back to your terminal."

There was no point in trying to explain, as far as Mr Clarke was concerned classified advertising stopped for nothing, bombs included. She logged back in. "Southingham Express, how may I help you?"

"Oh hello, I placed an advert yesterday for the sale of my car but you got the phone number wrong. All my calls will have been going to someone else."

Jenny groaned. "I'm so sorry, sir. Let me correct that for you. Would you like the advert to run this evening instead?"

"But today isn't the main car evening. That was yesterday. I needed to sell it before the MOT is due at the end of the week. I want some sort of compensation."

The rate she was going today she could forget the trip to Paris before she'd even started. "I'm sorry, I can put the advert in again for you, but if you wish to complain you'll need to write in to the supervisor."

"I don't want to write to your supervisor, I want you to sort it out."

Something inside Jenny snapped. She wasn't cut out to work in this kind of environment and if she was going down, she was going to do it in glorious style. "I'm very sorry Mr Simpson, would you like me to turn the clocks back twenty-four hours so that we can get it right first time?"

There was a long pause at the other end of the phone. She could almost hear Mr Simpson working out if what she said was possible. "I want to talk to your supervisor."

Jenny looked up to see Maureen going into the quiet room with a police officer. "I'm sorry, sir, I'm afraid that won't be possible at the moment. She's just been taken away by the police."

There was another silence. "I want to speak to someone in charge."

"Just hold the line and I'll put you through to our overall

boss. He's called Mr Rant, his first name's Ty, short for Tyrone."

"Southingham Express, how may I help you?"

"I've lost my Trixie and want to place an advert in case anyone finds her," said the tearful caller at the other end of the phone.

"Oh, I am sorry what exactly is Trixie?"

"She's my dog."

"And your name is?"

"She calls me Mummy."

"And is Mummy your actual name?"

"Don't be so ridiculous, it's Mrs Pamela Redmond."

"Well Mrs Redmond, I don't like to be insensitive, but have you tried the local takeaway to see if she's appeared on the menu?"

"Well, really. I want to speak to your ..."

"JENNY."

"I'm sorry Mrs Redmond, it's been nice talking to you. I think I have to go now."

"JENNY."

Jenny hung up her headset, thankful that it would be for the last time and headed for the boss's office. She knew she was going to be fired, still it had been fun and there was no way she'd have lasted here much longer.

"You called." She flashed her big blue eyes at Mr Clarke, and flicked her long blonde hair.

"JENNY," he shouted, while staring down at her cleavage. "How dare you talk to the customers of the Southingham Express like that?"

"I'm sorry," she beamed crossing her long slender legs which extended a long way out of her very short skirt. "Is there a problem?"

"I, well," Mr Clarke seemed to have lost his train of

thought. He looked away from her altogether. "You're fired. I'll pay you a month's notice but you can leave now."

"Oh well, there goes Paris." She got up, blew him a kiss and walked out. Never had it felt so good to be leaving a job behind. There would be enough money to tide her over until the new-year, when the short skirt should come in handy to get her another job. Maybe she'd try a car showroom this time.

She went shopping before going home, trying to brace herself for how to tell her parents that she'd lost another job. It was never easy to explain why it was that things always seemed to go wrong. She'd used the excuse that the boss had a problem with women, and the one that she had been covering for a friend and it was all a misunderstanding, when being fired from previous jobs. Admitting that she didn't suffer fools gladly would be far more honest, but her parents had such high expectations of her.

That was when it occurred to her. Never mind shopping, she couldn't afford a return, but she could buy a one way ticket to Paris and let the mini-skirt get her a job waitressing again. That way, not only would she see Philippe, but best of all, it would give her parents something more to complain about.

All she needed now was a flight to Paris.

TURNING THE TABLES

"Couldn't you maybe pop back at lunchtime?" Alison smiled hopefully at her husband as he picked up his overcoat.

"No good. Meetings all day. You know what Monday's are like. I won't be back until after seven." He stooped down and picked up the pile of mail off the mat and thrust it into her hands as he gave her a peck on the cheek. "All junk mail I suppose. Ruddy salesmen. We should sign up for that thing where they can't keep sending you this rubbish. Someone ought to teach them a lesson."

Then he was gone and Alison was left to look down at the pile of letters in her hand and wonder how she was going to fill the interminable boredom of another day. It would be much easier if she didn't still love Tony. If that were the case she could find herself a toy-boy or maybe a sugar daddy. She could find someone to add some spice to her life and maybe spoil her a bit. However, even after twenty-six years of marriage and despite his abruptness and insensitivity, with four grown children to call their own, Tony was still the man for her. Some of her friends worked, but what could she do? She'd been at home for the last twenty years and was convinced she had no skills to offer.

Retying her dressing gown, she caught a glimpse of herself in the hall mirror. She ran a hand through her lank sandy brown hair. She was too young to stagnate, although there wasn't much colour in her face at the moment, but then there didn't seem to be much colour in her life. She went through to the kitchen and mug of coffee in hand she sat down to look at the post. 'Test drive our new model', 'Arrange an appointment to review your finances', 'You too could have a new kitchen' and 'Furniture warehouse party – join us and drink champagne'. She let most of the letters fall off her legs onto the floor beside the chair and stared into her coffee. Now what? She couldn't ring any of the children. They'd be busy with work or lectures. She and Tony didn't have enough spare money for her to go shopping every day and these days all her friends seemed to work. It was easy to see how middle-aged women started drinking. A glass of wine now would be quite comforting.

She looked down at the remaining piece of paper on her lap. The picture showed an azure blue hatchback. Standing next to it was a happy smiling lady. Just the way she'd like to look and feel. Then Alison had an idea. Why shouldn't she test drive a new car? It didn't mean she had to buy it. Come to that, she'd be interested to hear someone else's views on her kitchen. She picked up the post off the floor and started to look at it in a new way. These weren't intrusions into their lives. They were opportunities to relieve the boredom. She fetched a biro and began to complete all the return cards, accepting every invitation.

Her first appointment was the following Tuesday.

The salesman couldn't have been more than twenty-five, armed with the latest technology and schooled in all the techniques to achieve a sale. "As you can see Mrs Davis, with our new door fronts you could rejuvenate your kitchen." The young man turned the computer screen towards her and showed her how her kitchen would look in a high gloss aubergine finish. His computer programme was amazing, allowing her to view her kitchen from every angle, complete with wall colours and curtains.

"May I just see the lime green one again?"

He typed a few commands into the keyboard and turned the screen back round. "If you sign up today I can offer you an extra 10% discount on the price."

"And with the oak finish?" They had been through about eleven different finishes so far. The young man happily changing the finish at every request. He didn't seem surprised that she was asking to see fittings very like the ones she already had.

He tapped away again.

"And perhaps if you could change the wall colour to powder blue and the curtains to blinds."

Alison sat back and looked at it. Yes, now she came to think about it her kitchen would look completely new if she just changed the colour of the walls and the curtain. Maybe she'd talk to Tony later about them doing some decorating.

"Thank you. Thank you very much. You have been most helpful. It's been a pleasure to meet you." She took a quick look at her watch. "Well I really must be getting on. If you can excuse me I have another appointment to get to at noon."

The salesman began to gather up his things. "I was hoping that maybe we could sort the order out before I left. Remember that extra discount. I won't be able to do these at the same price tomorrow."

"Yes, I'm sure that's the case. I couldn't possibly place an order without talking to my husband." She gave him a confident smile. "If you'll leave it here I will have a look at it with him when he gets home tonight and get back to you."

That afternoon when her day's appointments were out

of the way, Alison started to compose a letter. "Dear Editor, I made an amazing discovery today. Brightening up my kitchen doesn't have to be an expensive exercise..." She went on to briefly outline her ideas and addressed an envelope to her local paper. She'd still got some spare time so she decided to drop the letter round to their office by hand.

The following day Alison was up and ready to leave the house at the same time as Tony. She'd blown dry her hair and was smartly dressed in a trouser suit.

"Where are you off to so bright and early?"

"I'm test driving a car. I'm picking it up from the garage on the Stratford Road."

"Oh! What's wrong with your old one?"

She laughed. "Absolutely nothing at all. Don't worry, I'm not buying it. I just thought it would be fun to take the new model for a spin."

"Yes, of course." He shook his head. "I'll see you tonight." Tony looked confused, but Alison was grateful that he didn't ask any more questions.

As she drove away from the showroom, she couldn't help but think that the handbrake was in a slightly awkward position and the pedals were strangely off centre. She used the car for the weekly shopping and was frustrated by the height of the lip of the boot. Satisfied that this was not the car for her, she returned it to the showroom and set off home to put pen to paper.

"Dear Editor, today I had the fortune to drive the new 1.4 litre diesel hatchback...the designers have missed their market with this one..."

Alison looked in her diary. It would be the furniture store tomorrow. She was looking forward to considering the latest fashions in furnishing for her home and all over a nice glass of bubbly.

She was just putting pen to paper for the fourth day in a row when the telephone rang.

"Mrs Davis? It's Donald Baker here, the editor of the Billingbrook Express. I've been very interested to read the letters you've been sending us."

Alison's heart beat faster. Were they actually going to print one of her letters or was he ringing to ask her to stop writing to him. Surely, if he wasn't happy with her daily correspondence he'd have got someone else to ring. She took a deep breath.

"The thing is, I like your style of writing. I think it will connect with our readers. I was wondering if you'd like to start writing a daily column for the paper. An everyday consumer's angle on the world."

Alison couldn't have been more breathless if she'd just run around the block. "I... well, but I haven't got any experience."

Donald let out a deep roar of a laugh. "It seems to me that you've got all the experience you're ever going to need, from these letters. We'll pay you of course."

"Pay me!" Alison reached her left hand to pull a chair towards her and sat down. "You did just say 'pay me' didn't you?"

Donald laughed again. "Of course we'll pay you. I wouldn't expect you to do it for free. Why don't you come into my office tomorrow at ten so we can discuss the details?"

Alison grabbed her diary off the side. "I've got an appointment with a double glazing company then. Could we make it the afternoon?"

When Tony came home that evening, that day's post still lay unopened on the table. He started going through the pile. "Most of this can go straight in the bin."

"No!" shouted Alison, coming through from the kitchen carrying two glasses. "Don't see it as junk. See it as an opportunity." She smiled.

Tony took the glass. "But..."

"Here's to junk mail," she said raising her glass. Then kissing her bemused husband's cheek she added, "I've got something to tell you."

BETTER THAN ALL RIGHT

"I never thought growing old would be like this." Maureen swept strands of hair away from her face with the back of her hand. If she were a new car the brochure would describe the colour as 'silvio' or 'titanium', but whatever the fancy name, where she came from it was plain grey.

"You've got me, what more do you need?" Ted looked like a cartoon steam locomotive from heaving boxes down from the loft. His pistons propelled him in a direct line, forwards, straight over the pile of belongings she was carefully sorting out. He thrust the box onto the teetering pile of faded removals cartons. He'd brought all of those in since she'd asked him to stop to give her chance to catch up.

"You're falling behind."

"I'm not falling anywhere," she muttered to an ornate thimble celebrating the silver jubilee from 1977.

It wasn't hard to see how Ted had reached stalemate with their daughter. Like father, like daughter. Maureen sat back. She sighed as she wondered what Fiona might be doing.

"I thought I'd be surrounded by my grandchildren, taking days out to the zoo and the park, having someone to care for." She tried to imagine what her granddaughter would look like, but saw in her mind animations of Fiona's childhood, the uncompromising child who always succeeded because she never gave up. Every coin has two sides.

"Don't start going soft. If Fiona wanted to stay in touch, she knew where to find us. It isn't as though we've moved." He dabbed at the beads of sweat around his face with his handkerchief.

"Until now. What if she tries and we aren't here? Do you think we're right to move house? Should we just stay here?" She looked up at him, pleading with him to hear what she was really saying.

"Oh for goodness sake. Will you just snap out of it? You've said yourself this house is too big for the two of us." Ted pursed his lips as he looked at her.

Maureen hated that look and had to fight the instinct to shrink back.

Her voice quivered. "But what if there were more than two?"

"We haven't seen her for four years. What makes you think she's going to suddenly back down now?"

"It wasn't just her though, was it?" Maureen bit her lip and looked long and hard at her husband. 'For better or worse' that had been the promise. She sometimes wondered whether the wording should be changed. 'For thoughtful or thoughtless' maybe, and what was the opposite of stubborn? Her shoulders slumped as she went back to sorting through the box in front of her, laying each item out on the lounge carpet before working out whether it should join the 'skip' pile, the 'repack' hill or the 'not sure' mountain.

The air filled with fine particles of dust as Ted blew on the top of the next box that he'd just wrestled down from the loft.

"There's a cloth here." Maureen held the duster in his direction, knowing she was wasting her breath.

"It looks like a car boot sale in here. What's the point in

keeping all of this junk?"

"Memories." Maureen looked out into the garden at a passing butterfly.

"You've got me for memories. You don't need all this." He kicked his toe against a box containing a decorated vase. There was the mournful tinkle of braking china.

"That was my twenty-first birthday present from Aunt Joan." She felt a tear forming in the corner of her eye and brushed it away.

"There's no point us paying all that money for a skip if we're not going to fill it."

She wanted to say, 'Put your things in it then', but as she had for thirty-five years she held back and looked down at her grandmother's old silver milk jug that she was vigorously trying to rub clean.

"You should take that into the antique shop and see how much they'd give us for it. I might even have a look on eBay to see if there's anything similar." He turned and headed out of the room.

Maureen sniffed. "I thought it would pass down to the next generation. A family heirloom, from mother to daughter, to daughter, forever." She sighed heavily and put it next to the sugar bowl. Her granddaughter must be nine now. Maybe there were other children too.

She got up to put the kettle on, but paused to open the lid of the box that Ted had brought in before she did. Everything was wrapped neatly in newspaper from some long-gone year. She lifted the first item out of the box, carefully unwrapping its treasure. In front of her lay a misshapen clay house with a crooked chimney stack. She smiled sadly. It was meant to be a candle holder and had stood proudly on the sideboard for years, until one of Ted's little tidying-up sessions. She could still remember the day when Fiona brought it home from school, proudly presenting her mother with the present she'd made. The tears began to trickle down her cheeks again. How had it gone so wrong? The argument had been between Ted and Fiona. All she'd tried to do was help explain to Fiona what her father was saying. It just ended up with Fiona setting herself against both of them. This was her only child and she had spent the last four years pining for her.

Ted poked his head round the door. "I thought you were making a cuppa?"

Maureen felt the cogs fall into place. Enough was enough! She stood up from where she was bending. Pushing her shoulders back. Her cheeks felt flushed.

"I don't want to move to a bungalow. This is my home. I don't care that the garden is becoming a little overgrown. We'll get a gardener if we have to. We can afford it."

Ted's eyes widened. "Maureen, now don't let's be hasty."

"I haven't finished yet, Ted Byers. I'm not moving and I'm not throwing everything out just because you've gone to the trouble of hiring a skip. If you want to put your things in it then that's your business, but I'm not ready to part with my memories."

"But, Maureen..."

"Don't 'But, Maureen,' me. I've started now Ted and I'd appreciate it if you'd let me finish. You don't mean to be the way you are and I've put up with it for thirty-five years. If I thought you did it deliberately I'd have left you years ago. It's been, 'Yes, Ted', 'No, Ted', 'Anything you say, Ted'. Well it ends here! I'm going to find our daughter and while I've gone you can put this lot back in the loft for me to look at when I'm ready." With that, Maureen picked up the little pottery house and marched out of the room.

She got as far as the kitchen before slumping into one of the chairs, her head in her hands. She'd heard from friends that Fiona was moving, but she had no idea of her new address. The internet was probably the place to start, but that was Ted's domain. Ted had always been the one doing things on the computer. She used email and knew how to listen to radio programmes, but she wasn't very familiar with it.

She crept from the kitchen to the study, her confidence ebbing away. She turned the computer on and sat back, waiting for it to whir into life. She stared at the internet page, moving the cursor around the screen and wondering what to look for.

She'd been transfixed for about five minutes before finally taking a deep breath. "Ted!"

He came to the door still looking several inches shorter than he had before.

She searched for the right words. She didn't want to back down completely. She still needed to make a stand, but she needed Ted to work with her. "I'm sorry. I may have been a little hasty. I do still need your help."

Ted smiled. It wasn't a smile of victory, more of relief. He moved over to where she was and very gently put his hand over hers. "I..." he faltered and cleared his throat. "I had no idea. I'm sorry." He guided her hand to the search bar and typed in 'electoral roll'.

Maureen felt closer to Ted than she had in years. Once they had been a team. That was what drew them together, gliding across the ice in harmony. He lifted her as they spun. She spiralled barely touching his hand. She smiled.

As he typed Fiona's name, she wondered how he knew where to search. It was so easy to let him take charge. That had always been one of her problems. But as they sat together now, he was different. There was none of the orders issued or the thoughtless comments.

They narrowed their search down to one very likely looking address and phone number, which Ted checked by finding Fiona's husband listed at the same address.

"I think I'd rather drive over there than phone."

"Would you like me to come? It's quite a way on your own. I could wait in the car."

Maureen patted his shoulder. "No, thank you. I appreciate the offer, but I think I'd like to do the next bit myself."

Ted didn't argue. He simply nodded.

#

Fiona was ironing when Lucy came home from school. The nine-year-old looked up delighted at her mother.

"I've got something for you. You've got to close your eyes."

Fiona put the iron down and closed her eyes.

"Now hold out your hands."

Fiona put her open hands in front of her, waiting to see what surprise Lucy had in store. An object was placed into her hands and Fiona felt her way around the edges. She could feel a misshapen handle and a rough base, with smooth slightly sloping sides.

"Can I open my eyes yet?"

"Ok."

Lucy's face was beaming and in Fiona's hands was a lumpy, off-centre mug on which was painted 'I love Mum' under the shiny glaze.

"It's for you," said Lucy proudly.

"Darling, it's beautiful." Fiona's tears were staining her perfectly made-up face. She reached a tissue off the side and dabbed her eyes before hugging her daughter. Her heart leapt with pride at what Lucy had done. She placed the slightly wobbly mug in the centre of the mantelpiece for all to see.

It was a week later when Fiona was sitting with a glass of wine, looking at the mug and thinking of her own mother. It was hard to believe that she hadn't been in touch. She knew Peter was right when he said it took two, but the argument had only ever really been with her dad. She felt rejected by her mum. She couldn't imagine ever losing touch with her own beautiful daughter. She sipped her wine wondering if her parents were still in the same house.

Fiona didn't hear the doorbell. The first she knew was when Peter poked his head around the door. "It's for you, love."

"What is?"

"You've got a visitor. She's in the hall."

She swung round to put her glass on the table, spilling wine down her shirt as she went. "Oh bother." She began to dab at her top as she went towards the hall. She wasn't used to having visitors, at least not ones who came unannounced. When she opened the door and saw her mother standing there, she froze.

"I brought you this." Maureen thrust the crooked house towards her.

Fiona stood with her mouth open, her hands outstretched towards the clay house.

Lucy came running into the hall and stopped when she saw the pair of them. She looked at the little house and grinned. "Hey Mum, it's not as good as the mug I made you."

Fiona laughed. "Why don't you go and get the mug to show to Grandma." She looked up at her mum. "Why don't you come in."

Lucy clutched her hand as though no time had passed at all.

Maureen was crying as she followed Lucy. "Your mother made it for me when she was about your age."

"And you've still got it?"

"I'm sure your mum will still have this mug in another twenty-five years as well. Hopefully you two won't have lost touch." Then letting go of Lucy's hand, she hugged her daughter. "It's been a long time. Can we start again?"

Fiona could only nod through the haze of tears.

Lucy looked up at her father. "Is Mummy all right?"

"Yes, darling, I rather think she is."

"Better than all right," sobbed Fiona, smiling at her daughter through the tears. "Better than all right."

A LITTLE PIECE OF HEAVEN

"Davy, you've been sitting around the house for weeks. It's about time you did something." Jennie picked up a red velvet cushion off the chair and plumped it back into shape.

"Oh, I am doing something, Jennie, darling. I am doing something." Davy pressed the off button and put the remote control down on the side.

"You mean other than sitting with your feet on the coffee table, drinking beer and watching television?"

"I, my dear woman, am going to be the next Duncan Bannatyne, the next Richard Branson." He raised his arm in an expansive gesture. "Today Billingbrook, tomorrow the world."

"And you're going to do that by sitting on our settee?" Jennie was fed up with having her husband under her feet. Ever since Davy had been made redundant from his carpet fitting job, he had barely left the house. She knew at fifty-five his age was against him in the employment market and she didn't want to be too hard on her beloved husband. However, his redundancy money wasn't going to last forever and the small amount she earned from her part-time job wasn't going to pay all the bills. She'd asked for more hours, but times were hard and no one really had work available.

"No, really, darling," he said, swinging his feet around and getting up. He was showing more purpose than she had seen him move his slightly flabby figure with for years.

He picked her up and swung her around. "We're going to be rich and we don't even need to do the lottery."

"How many of those cans of beer have you had, Davy?"

"It's not the beer talking. It's a miracle."

Jennie stood with her hands on her well-developed hips. "And since when have we been subject to miracles at number 6 Windsor Crescent?"

Davy looked at his watch. "Since about 3 o'clock. Give or take fifteen minutes. Your mother was a medium wasn't she and you've always said you thought you might have picked up some of her powers."

"Davy, what are you up to?" Jennie frowned. She might have said that, but she wasn't sure she really believed it.

He grinned, kissed her full on the lips and then went through to the den calling behind him, "All in good time, Mystic Jennie, all in good time."

Jennie shook her head and went back to the kitchen, leaving Davy to fiddle about on the computer. She'd long since learned when he was in one of these moods that he wouldn't tell her a word about his idea until he was ready.

Half an hour later he poked his head around the door. "I'm just nipping out to the shops for an hour or so. Is there anything you need?"

Jennie raised an eye-brow. What was he up to? "No, love, I'll see you later."

Davy maintained his secrecy for the rest of that day and most of the following one, before eventually calling her through into the den. "I'm ready to reveal the way to make our millions."

"And I'm ready to spend them, but I'm not expecting that to happen anytime soon."

"Oh, ye of little faith." He removed a tea-towel that was carefully placed covering the computer screen, to reveal a page of eBay, the online sales and auction site.

"Second hand goods! You're never going to make millions out of second-hand goods."

"That, dear lady, depends on what the second-hand goods are. We are not selling any old junk. We are selling 'a little piece of heaven'."

"We're selling what?"

"A little piece of heaven. You can have a piece of the Lord's damask table cloth." He picked up a small bag containing an inch square of material. "You can have a segment of angel harp string." He picked up another bag and passed it to Jennie. "Or you can have a dried grape from the feast of heaven."

"Davy, even I can see they're Tesco's raisins."

"But what if you hadn't seen the packet on the desk? What then? All it needs is a little faith."

"And how precisely are people to believe that you've obtained these things?"

"Through a very clever medium. And that's where you come in."

"I'm supposed to have secured all these goods for you from the 'other side'!"

"Just think for a minute, Jennie. There are people out there selling pieces of turf from football pitches. Where have they come from? How do you know they didn't grow them in their back garden? There are dealers selling famous people's autographs that the dealer has done themselves. Better still, there are people out there openly selling 'an acre of the moon'. What is that about? No one really owns the moon. No one can visit or build on their acre and yet people buy them. And why do they buy them?"

Davy's face was alive and excited for the first time in as long as Jennie could remember.

"They buy them because they want something special. Something no one else has got. So why won't people buy 'a little piece of heaven'? Let's face it, if they are looking for pieces of heaven in the first place, they either want a present that is different or they already believe it might be out there. We'll just be meeting a demand."

"And what happens when Trading Standards start to ask questions?"

"That's the beauty of it. How many Trading Standards officers have visited heaven to know whether these things are real?"

"You mean the ones that haven't seen the Tesco's bags!"

"Come on, Jennie. If you can't have faith in a money making idea, what can you believe in? As of five o'clock this evening we're in business and Mystic Jennie is selling 'a little piece of heaven' to anyone who wants to buy."

Jennie shook her head. As long as Davy didn't do any real harm and didn't get arrested then at least it would give him something to do. Mind you, even if he did get arrested, at least he wouldn't be sitting in front of the television with his endless cans of beer. All things considered perhaps it wasn't such a bad idea.

REVERSING THE TREND

"I didn't order..." Sandra's voice trailed off as she stared at the chocolate cheesecake in the top box of shopping. Then she remembered feeling sorry for herself and filling her online trolley with lots of treats. She lifted the cheesecake and looked in dismay at the chocolate mousses underneath.

"Is everything all right, love?" The delivery driver asked as he handed her the electronic scanner.

"Yes... fine." She couldn't admit to a stranger that she was a sad middle-aged woman having a crisis. She signed for the shopping and carried it through to the kitchen.

All middle-aged women were a little overweight, Sandra reasoned. Who was going to notice if she was carrying a few extra pounds? Besides, she did need cheering up.

She put away the rest of the shopping and piled up the cheesecake, mousses, chocolates and truffles wondering what to do next. If she put them in the fridge the rest of the family might find them and they were hers. As she moved the eggs aside to hide things behind them she felt the first twinge of guilt. Part of the reason she was feeling down was because of the extra weight she was already carrying. How was this going to help? She put the thought out of her mind as she took out a spoon to try the new variety of mousse that had been on special offer. It wasn't even that nice. Maybe that was why it was reduced. If she just had one of the others to take the taste away...

Two spoons in Sandra stopped and stared at it. That one wasn't particularly nice either. She moved them back in front of the egg carton and turned toward the box of chocolates. She could hear them calling 'eat me', but what if they were a disappointment too? That would be dreadful.

Turning the box over, Sandra looked at the best before date. She didn't need to eat them just yet. What if she were to look at this differently? She went and looked in the hall mirror and tried to imagine what she might look like if her jeans weren't too tight with a midriff spilling unceremoniously over the top. Willpower, she just needed a little willpower and maybe an incentive too.

She busied herself cooking dinner whilst an inner argument played out in her head.

'You're not strong enough to do this and besides it doesn't really matter.'

'What if you need hospital treatment and they won't treat you because you're fat?'

'You aren't very overweight. Only just into the obese category. They'd still treat you if you needed it.'

'Think how much easier it would be on your joints if you weren't carrying the extra.'

'Go on, lick the spoon, you know you're hungry and you want to. It will taste nice.'

She put the radio on to drown out the gremlins and finished cooking.

"I'm starving. What's for dinner, Mum?" Tom sauntered into the kitchen, texting as he came in.

"Smells delicious, darling," her husband Pete said, giving her a peck on the cheek. Before sitting down at the table.

"There's cheesecake for afters, if any of you are still hungry," she said once the spaghetti Bolognese was cleared away.

There was a chorus of 'Yes please' from around the table, so with a small pang of disappointment Sandra got up and went to the fridge, ferreting behind the vanilla yoghurts until she could get the cheesecake out. She took one last lingering look as she cut it into pieces and passed it out to the rest of the family. Then she started loading the dishwasher whilst they ate, so she wouldn't have to think about the fact that she wasn't having any. She knew they wouldn't notice. If she changed her mind there were still two pieces back in the fridge.

The next step was to get on the scales. Sandra had been avoiding them for a while now. She knew it wouldn't be good news, but she had to start somewhere. She braced herself and thought of all the clothes that no longer fitted. It would be lovely to wear her summer dresses again in a few months and not have her tee shirts feel so tight. Two stone wasn't too much if you said it quickly. She wondered if the weight would sound better if she measured it in kilograms.

Back in the kitchen she took a bag of sugar out of the cupboard. Everywhere she went she was carrying fourteen of these that she didn't need. No wonder she didn't feel so good. She sipped her tea and thought about the cheesecake. If she didn't actually tell anyone she was dieting then it wouldn't matter if she failed. 'You'd still be letting yourself down,' a little voice whispered in her ear.

With a deep sigh she served the rest of the cheesecake out the following day and went to stack the dishwasher. This wasn't going to be easy.

"That was lovely, darling," Pete said, taking her in his arms when he left the table. "I was thinking, at the weekend, why don't I go and see if I can buy you some of those champagne truffles you like so much?"

Sandra broke into a sheepish grin and led him into the other room. She picked up the box of chocolates and the box of truffles. "You could just give me these."

"Do I still get all the credit?" he asked, laughing.

She nodded slowly and then looking up at him said, "These chocolates are for when I've lost the first stone and these..." she turned the truffles over to check the date again, "... are for when I hit my ideal weight." There, she'd said it. Now she couldn't go back on her decision and it gave her six months to achieve her goal.

AN IMPORTANT DECISION

"I can't believe that this time tomorrow we'll be on a beach in Spain," said Marcie bouncing up and down as she spoke. She was literally tingling with excitement. "It'll be our first foreign holiday together."

Gary sneered at her. "Hello, my name's Marcie and my specialist subject is stating the bleedin' obvious."

Marcie stopped bouncing. "There's no need to be like that, Gary. I know you've been abroad a lot, but I haven't." It had been his worldly wisdom which had first made her notice him. Somehow it made him seem so cool next to the other blokes she met. That and his cheeky smile, though she didn't seem to see so much of that these days.

"Yeah, well. Just go downstairs out of me way while I pack. You don't want me to forget somat do you?"

Marcie thought he was leering rather than grinning. It gave her an uneasy feeling. She shivered slightly, remembering the look he'd given her when she gave him the parcel she'd picked up from his mate Gavin's kid brother the week before.

"I'll make us a cup o' tea." She almost danced down the stairs recovering some of her mood by thinking of drinking sangria overlooking the sea. She'd been to Spain once before on a family holiday about 12 years ago. She must have been about 10, but it was the best holiday she could ever remember, even so, going away with Gary, her very own boyfriend was going to be way better.

They'd only moved in together the previous month, but

Marcie was certain that Gary was THE one, despite everything her mother had said. Of course now her mum was on her own she was bound to worry about her little girl. The kettle belched steam like an overenthusiastic dragon and she pressed the faulty rocker switch to stop it.

She went back upstairs carrying two mugs of steaming tea and gently pushed the bedroom door open with her back. Suddenly it slammed shut again and the scalding tea spilt down her wrists.

"I told you to stay downstairs, you stupid cow."

Marcie bit her bottom lip as she felt a heaving sob rise up from nowhere. Gary needed this holiday so much. He'd been working all hours, often going back in the evening. She told herself it was the pressure and it wasn't his fault as she went down to the kitchen to run her hands under the cold water. Money had been so tight recently, she knew he was worried. He hadn't meant to do it, any more than he'd meant to hit her the night he came back from Gavin's, drunk. It would all be different when they were away together.

#

"Two of you travelling?"

Marcie handed their tickets to the check-in lady at the airport and grinned at Gary.

"Did you pack the bags yourself?"

"Yes," she said as Gary stood looking around the terminal behind them.

"And are you carrying any of these items?" the check-in clerk indicated the picture symbols attached to the front of the counter.

"No," Marcie said, then hesitated a moment. She had no idea what Gary had packed and he wasn't taking any notice at all. She chided herself for being ridiculous and smiled at the lady.

She took their boarding cards and they headed through to Departures. She could feel the butterflies in her stomach and when Gary suggested they get a drink it seemed like a great idea to steady her nerves. She gazed in the windows of the stores as they passed, wishing she could do more than window shop.

It didn't seem like five minutes before they'd landed the other end and were trying to pull their bags off the carousel onto the trolley.

"Here you push this, Marce," Gary instructed as they made their way through all the arrival processes.

"Why me?" She hated it when he abbreviated her name. He said it was endearment, but he always did it when he was ordering her about.

"Just do it," he said scowling at her.

Marcie thought how funny it was that when she walked past customs officers she felt nervous even though she'd only got her holiday stuff. She relaxed when they came out into the Arrivals hall to find their Holiday Rep. Gary was smiling for the first time and she thought he was finally starting to relax.

She'd made sure she'd got one of those cheap phone packages for calling from abroad before they set off and while Gary went to find the gents, she rang her mate Jo to tell her they'd arrived. She would have rung her Mum, but it was a bit late and she presumed her mum would have gone to bed. She was forgetting it was an hour earlier back home.

Where they were staying wasn't too far from the airport and they were one of the first drop offs. It was a self-catering place, basic but ok.

"I'm glad we're here. I'm tired after the travelling."

Marcie kicked off her shoes and lugged her case onto the bed to unpack.

"Why don't you stay here, love, and I'll go and do a recce and then bring us back a pizza or somat?"

Gary hardly ever called her 'love'. It was great to see the real Gary coming out. She always said he could be really considerate. "Thanks, Gary. I'll unpack then."

"I'll do mine," he snapped, taking her by surprise. He lifted his case into the corner and checked the lock. She frowned, but if he'd brought a present for her then she supposed it made sense.

She waited a couple of hours for him, but he didn't come back. He'd probably got talking to someone in the bar and lost track of time. She wasn't really hungry so in the end she went to bed. By the time she got up in the morning the sun was shining and Gary was snoring soundly. She had no idea what time he'd come in. She opened the shutters.

"What the hell are you doing?" Gary sat up suddenly. "Turn that bleeding light off, I'm trying to sleep here."

"I was only..."

"Well don't," he rolled over as she pulled the shutters back into place. She sighed heavily. It was decision time. She could either sit here as she did at home, or she could go out and enjoy the sunshine and find some breakfast. She could hear her mum's words echoing after Dad died. 'I'll be ok, love. I always made sure I could still do things on my own.' She made a decision, her mum was right. It was Marcie's holiday too. She scribbled a note on the back of a flyer for jet ski hire and went out as quietly as she could, taking her stuff for the pool with her.

It was 4pm before Gary joined her. "Where've you been?" He looked annoyed.

"I had a walk around and then I've been here listening

to my iPod." She pulled the earphone out of her ear. She'd only had one in so she could hear what was going on around the pool.

"Well I'm hungry. Let's get some food, my treat."

She shrugged. It had been a while since breakfast and she hadn't bothered with lunch. She gathered her belongings and followed him. With Gary it was no good suggesting they try any of the local food. That was never going to happen, so they settled themselves in a place selling good old English fry ups, alongside some local dishes. He ordered a litre of wine, so Marcie was surprised when he asked for a beer as well. She presumed he was planning to drink both. As the meal progressed he kept filling her glass and she was sure he was only drinking the beer, even though he'd put a little of the wine in his glass. They sat there for ages and after a while the wine had really gone to her head.

"Looks like we'd better get you back," he said and indicated he wanted the bill. She was stunned when he pulled his wallet out to pay and it was stuffed with notes. He'd told her to only get him €200 before they came. He must have gone to the cashpoint.

She staggered back to the apartment with Gary's help. She couldn't remember feeling quite this wobbly from alcohol before. She fell into bed and was out like a light. She woke up needing a drink of water a few hours later and was surprised to find she was on her own and Gary was nowhere about. It was too late to ring home and she really wasn't feeling great, so she went back to bed.

The next day started much the same. Gary was asleep where he should be and, despite the hangover, she wanted to go out. She hesitated, the holiday was so they could spend time together, but she didn't want to waste the whole day. She'd imagined they'd be going on trips out and lying by the pool together. She remembered some of the places they'd been to on the holiday when she was a kid. It made her mind up. She got her things together and went out. This time she got a bus to the next town and had a look round. She had breakfast in a place that had a sign saying it was available to rent. Not just rooms so people could stay there, the whole restaurant! She started to dream what it would be like to have her own taverna and what she'd do differently. Her mum had always worked in catering and having her own place had been her mum's dream when she was younger. Marcie rang her mum as she ate her breakfast.

"I've found us a great place to work, Mum." Her mum laughed as Marcie told her all about it. Marcie realised she was relaxed and really enjoying herself, even though Gary wasn't there.

She was back by the pool when he found her about 4.30pm. The pattern was much the same as the day before. She didn't dare ask him where he'd been. She knew how he'd react. Then she had a thought. If he did it tonight, she'd follow him. They went back to the same café to eat. He ordered wine for her again, but she decided she wasn't going to drink much of it, but she needed him to think she had. Her chance came when he went off to the gents and she was able to tip most of it into the plant behind her. She ended up drinking only a couple of glasses, but the odd thing was she felt just as drunk.

He took her back to the apartment and she was asleep long before there was time for her to plan how to follow him. The pattern continued the following day. She caught the bus back to 'her taverna' and sat daydreaming. She even went as far as writing down the number of the agent from the sign. She knew she'd never do anything with it, but the lightness she felt, as she sat in the dappled sunshine imagining the changes she'd make to the menu, was something she'd almost forgotten.

Lying by the pool, she began to form a plan for the evening. The first part was to have a large late lunch so that she wouldn't be hungry.

When they sat down in their usual place she went through the motions of ordering both food and wine, but before it even arrived she was moving to the next stage of the plan.

"I don't feel very well."

"Should have stayed in bed like I did." Gary seemed quite pleased with himself, even though he wasn't seeing anything much of the resort by daylight.

"Maybe I've had too much sun." She made a point of mopping her forehead with the paper napkin and then headed for the ladies, wobbling slightly as she went.

By the time she got back the food was there and she deliberately moved it around her plate without eating any.

"Here have a drink. It'll make you feel better," Gary said, filling her glass almost brim full with wine.

"I think I'll leave it thanks. Maybe I should go back and lie down. I'll wait till you finish."

"Yeah, I'll walk you back."

She couldn't believe that at no point in the week had Gary complained that she wasn't up to going out with him in the evenings. He'd not even made many snide remarks about her doing her own thing during the day. She had an uneasy feeling that something was wrong; very wrong.

Back at the apartment she stripped down to her tee shirt and climbed under the sheet that covered the bed.

"You don't need me here do you?" Gary didn't look as

though he planned to stay even if she did say 'yes'.

"No, I'll see you later."

"Yeah, sleep well." And with that he'd gone. She heard some scuffling outside the apartment door. "It's ok, love, just dropped me wallet."

Marcie frowned. There it was again; 'love'. She listened to his steps going down to street level and then went to the window to see which way he headed, opening the shutters only far enough to allow her to see out. He'd headed to the town they were on the edge of. It would be impossible to follow him, but she could at least go out and say she felt better so she thought she'd join him, if she could find which bar he was in.

She dressed in more comfortable clothes than she'd normally wear for a night out. She didn't want to attract any unwelcome attention while she was looking for him and who knew how many bars she'd have to look in first? She picked up her bag, quickly ran a comb through her hair and headed for the door. She turned the handle and pulled it towards her. Nothing happened.

"What the..."

The door was locked. Gary had locked her in and taken the key with him. She was a prisoner. She pulled the door again. Perhaps the handle was stuck. Surely he wouldn't do that. Maybe he was doing it for her safety, but what if she had to get out in a hurry if there were a problem? She frowned deeply and sat on the edge of the bed. Gary had locked her in. Gary didn't want her to follow him. She shook her head. Surely she was wrong. She got up and tried the door again. Still nothing. She turned and saw Gary's still locked case in the corner of the room. As the week was going, it was very unlikely that it had a present for her in it. She looked at the four digit combination. It was set to all the zeros. He wasn't likely to be back for hours. What numbers might he use? She tried the year he was born and then the day and month of his birthday. It didn't move. There was nothing else for it. She sat on the floor in front of the case and started with 0-0-0-1.

"Please, God, don't let it be 9-9-9-9." She turned it to that just in case. She laughed and went back to doing the numbers in turn. 0-2-3-1, 0-2-3-2. She slumped back against the wall. This could take all night. She looked at her watch, it was only 7pm. She'd probably got all night. An hour and a half later she was up to 2-4-5-3 and decided to ring Jo. Maybe if she talked to her friend she'd be able to make some sense of it all.

"Marcie, just come home. Get on the next flight out of there and come home."

"I can't. I've got no money and besides I can't get out of the apartment."

"Tomorrow then. I'll lend you the money."

"But it might all be ok."

"Marcie, will you listen to yourself? It is clearly not ok. Come home. Do you want me to ring your mum?"

"NO." Marcie almost shouted at her friend. "Sorry," she said more quietly. "It's just..." but she couldn't finish the sentence. What was it just? She didn't want her mum to know she was right? She didn't want to feel stupid? She wanted it all to be ok and there to be a reasonable explanation. "Look, Jo, I'll ring you tomorrow. I'll be ok, right."

2-4-5-4, 2-4-5-5.

She carried on for another hour or so, but by 10pm and having got to 5-7-4-7 she had still not opened the case. She reset it to the zeros and went to bed.

It was the fifth day of the holiday. Nothing much had

changed. Marcie's tan was developing nicely and she had totally fallen in love with the neighbouring town. She had been trying to work out a plan for later that day when it came to her. Around 3pm she headed for the café that Gary had taken to going to and ordered both food and drink. She knew when he didn't find her by the pool he was likely to head there. The wine tasted good as she relaxed over her paella. She'd only ordered a small carafe and was just starting her second glass when she heard him.

"What are you doing here?"

"I was hungry and I thought this way you'd find me easily." She was trying to sound as charming as possible, but held her glass close, quickly pouring the remaining wine from the carafe. He sat opposite to her and clicked his fingers to attract attention. She hated when he did that.

"I thought I might come with you to the bar tonight," she tried to be casual. It was more than half way through the week and so far she hadn't been out past 8pm.

"Yeah, great," he said but from the way he was staring at the mini-skirted blonde going by in the street she knew he hadn't heard a word she'd said.

She sipped the wine slowly, watching him. Waiting for him to talk. He didn't.

"So where are we going?" she asked after an uncomfortably long silence.

"I thought you were ill," he said picking up a chip.

Slowly and patiently she said, "No, I'm fine."

"I'm meeting some of the lads to watch the football, you'll be bored."

"Right," she didn't know what to say to avoid a scene. "I'll just go back then shall I?"

"There's a good girl."

She could feel her cheeks flushing. This was not the

holiday she'd had in mind. She looked at him closely. He wasn't even that good looking. She wondered if she could go to the bar and meet someone else, but quickly dismissed that as she thought of his jealous rages.

She listened to his steps walking away from the apartment. Of course, he'd walked her back again. She let the quiet continue for ten minutes and then got off the bed.

5-7-4-8, 5-7-4-9... 6-2-7-1, 6-2-7-2 she heard a slight click as the tumblers of the lock fell into place. Bingo.

Her heart was racing as she laid the case down flat and started to run the zip round the edge. She memorised the position the case had been in and that of the closed zip. She couldn't afford to take any chances. She was ready to open the lid. Her palms were sweating. What was she expecting to find? She had no idea but she certainly thought there was going to be something more than dirty underwear. She listened, but there was no sound outside. She lifted the lid and leant it back against the wall. Carefully laid across the top were jeans and beach shorts. She lifted the edge and gasped. Underneath was more money in euro bills than she'd ever seen in her life. She thought of the broken kettle and the times he'd shouted at her for spending too much. She frowned. She ran her hands round the case and felt a plastic bale. She moved things aside to get a closer look.

"Shit." She knew exactly what she was looking at. Well not exactly, obviously there were different types of white powder, but it certainly wasn't talc! And there was more than one. She gulped. Her hands were shaking as she started to put everything back into the case in exactly the same position she'd found it. She zipped the case and reset the lock to all the zeros then stood it in the corner where it had been before. She was cold and trembling as she went to the bathroom and threw up. She had brought the case into the country. It had been Marcie who pushed the trolley. Marcie who checked it in. Marcie who said she'd packed it herself. She retched again, but nothing more came up.

She wanted to go home. Not to the flat she shared with Gary, really home. To her mum's house. To the little bedroom with butterflies on the wallpaper. She'd promised to ring Jo, but what could she say? 'My boyfriend's a drug dealer and I'm terrified.' She needed a plan. She trusted Jo, they'd been mates since starting school. Jo would help. She sat with her head in her hands trying to think what to do next.

"Jo."

"Marcie, you all right? You sound different. Gary's not been knocking you about again has he?"

She could hear the anger in her friend's voice and it gave her courage. "No, nothing like that." She felt the tears start to fall as she began to tell Jo what had happened. "I need to turn him in, Jo, but I don't know what to do. Not here. I don't want to do it here."

"What if he's sold it all though?"

"I dunno. I hadn't thought of that. There's a lot."

Jo agreed to talk to the police at home and ask them what Marcie should do. Marcie sat fidgeting with a piece of paper. She wanted to write down what actions she needed to take, she was scared of losing the thoughts, but if Gary saw it there'd be real trouble. Most of all she had to stay calm and not let on that she knew anything. What was that saying that everyone seemed to put on mugs now 'Keep calm and carry on', yeah, that was it and it was exactly what she needed to do. She couldn't leave and go home early. She'd got to stay another two days and she'd have to meet up with Gary each afternoon or he'd be suspicious, or angry, or both! She wondered if she still loved him, but right now she was too numb to know. What if she turned him in and he came after her? Or his mates? What was she getting into?

She lay awake listening. She could hear drunken revelry outside the apartment, but strangely didn't want to be part of it. It was like she was suddenly older and all this partying wasn't for her anymore. She needed a plan. What if...

She woke with a start. She could hear clattering around the apartment. Her heart was thumping. She didn't move. Then she heard the sound of a case zip opening. Gary, she presumed and breathed a little more deeply. She didn't want him to know she was awake. She steadied her breathing and hoped that her heart was not as loud as it sounded thudding in her ears. Eventually she heard him climb into bed next to her and shift position. She rolled onto her side and lay quietly in the darkness.

She lay by the pool the next day, groggy and catching up on the sleep she hadn't got the night before. Her phone was tucked under the cushion by her ear and it made her jump when it vibrated.

"It's me, Jo, can you talk?" Jo was almost whispering as though there were people her end she didn't want to hear what she said. Marcie smiled to think of her friend being all conspiratorial in an otherwise empty house. Then she realised it was daytime so she was probably at work.

"Yeah, give me a minute." Marcie looked around, she hadn't got to know anyone, but for all she knew they might know Gary. She picked up her bag and started walking down the road towards the bus stop. "Ok."

"There'll be officers waiting at Heathrow to pick him up. You need to make sure he's got his own case and that you've got yours and nothing's been put in it. They'll pull you both in. Try to make it look as though they haven't been tipped off."

"Then what?"

"They'll let you go."

"But I can't go back to the flat." Marcie drew a breath in sharply. "Jo, I can't ever go back to the flat."

"Ok, we'll work something out. Anyway, the police want to talk to you too. Can I give them your number?"

They rang that afternoon not long before she was expecting Gary to arrive. She was sweating as they talked to her. "What? Can you say that again?"

"We'll need you to testify against him at the trial."

"I don't know. It won't be safe. I need to think."

"We'll call you again tomorrow."

"Make it early. Early morning will be good. It's not safe at this time of day. He's coming."

She hung up without waiting for a reply and slipped the phone into her pocket, hoping Gary hadn't seen.

#

It was now the last full day and Marcie couldn't sleep. Gary hadn't been back long, but she waited until he was snoring before she got up.

She decided to hire a car. Gary didn't need to know, and besides there were some places she wanted to check out before she went home. Despite what might lie ahead, she felt as though anything was possible. Planning a future on her own might be scary, but nothing could be as bad as what she was leaving behind. Her mobile phone rang and she pulled off the road.

The greeting was brief, it was the police call she'd been expecting. She took a deep breath and nodded to herself, she was ready. "I need a safe flat while I'm back in England

and a new identity, but yes, I'll testify." She let out a long breath and slumped in the seat as she cancelled the call from the police.

Tomorrow and the thought of going through customs was far too scary to think about. For now she'd focus on what her life could look like when it was all over. Marcie dialled her mother.

"Hi, Mum. It turns out you were right. How would you like to run your own restaurant and live in the sun into the bargain... with me!"

She heard the delighted laughter in her mother's voice as she asked Marcie if she were serious.

"Yes, Mum, I've made an important decision. It's time for me to take a leaf out of your book and get on with my life... without Gary. There's a taverna I've seen that's available to rent. I'm thinking of taking on the lease and I wondered if you'd like to join me."

PRINCESS ISABELLA AND THE TALE OF THE THREE WISHES

Once upon a time, there was a beautiful princess. She had buck teeth and thick-lensed glasses, but she was a beautiful princess none-the-less. Isabella had tried to find her prince charming, but it hadn't gone well, so she booked herself on a city break to Nice.

Normally, fairy godmothers aren't the sort of people you see much of. They appear occasionally for birthdays and Christmases. Generally they're conspicuous by their absence. You can imagine Isabella's surprise as she sat enjoying a glass of wine in the sunshine, when who should arrive, but her fairy godmother, a tall, elegant woman, who oozed brisk efficiency.

"Darling, it's been ages," said her godmother, kissing the air on either side of Isabella's face with undue enthusiasm.

"About five years three months and twelve days if we are being precise," said Isabella sharply. She'd never managed to get the whole 'fairy godmother thing' working for her and was not particularly keen on small talk.

"Oo touchy, touchy," said her fairy godmother in a mock scold. "I've been busy with my other clients. I don't just look after you. How are things? How's Gareth?"

"Gareth?" Asked Isabella confused. "Who's Gareth?"

"Oh dear," said her godmother, "I must be getting your file mixed up with somebody else. Why don't we start at the beginning? The very beginning."

"I've heard it's a very good place to start," Isabella shot her godmother a look of daggers. "Now let me see. You turned up at my Christening and gave me 'wisdom'. Then there was my eighteenth birthday when you gave me 'wealth', then my twenty-first you added 'success'."

"Well that's fantastic," said her godmother, but Isabella wasn't finished.

"The special occasions when you might have given me 'happiness', 'companionship' and 'love' you must have been otherwise engaged. Perhaps you were busy with one of your other files."

"Ah," said her godmother a little less enthusiastically. "So there's no Gareth?"

"No," said Isabella starting to get cross, "there's no Gareth, in fact there's no anybody!" Isabella felt her eyes moistening and her fairy godmother looked as though she was beginning to feel that in some small way she might be responsible.

"Oh, darling," she gushed, "there's no need for tears. I'm here now, I can put it right. You're still only in your twenties."

"I'm thirty-five," sniffed Isabella. "How many single princesses do you know who are thirty-five?" She paused and could see her godmother counting. "And that doesn't include the divorced ones."

Her godmother looked deflated and stopped counting. "Well none then, except you. Unless you count Mad Meg, but I'm guessing you didn't want to be compared to her."

"So how are you going to put that right?"

Isabella's godmother rummaged through her handbag. "I've got a 'get out of jail free card' if that helps?"

"No," snapped Isabella.

Her fairy godmother searched through the other

pockets in her bag and pulled out a tatty pink envelope. She handed it to Isabella tentatively. "I suppose you could have this. I've been saving it for an emergency."

The envelope was stamped in large, solid black letters 'CAUTION – HANDLE WITH CARE'. "What exactly are you giving me?" Isabella sounded considerably less truculent.

"Open it, darling. It's quite safe." Her fairy godmother paused, "at this stage!"

Isabella withdrew a piece of paper and started to read aloud from the very grand writing.

"To whom it may concern..."

"That's you," said her godmother.

Isabella coughed and started again more forcefully. *"To whom it may concern, it is hereby decreed by the Guild of Fairy Godmothers, that the holder of this paper shall be entitled to the granting of three wishes entirely of their own choosing."* Isabella cast her eyes down to read the incredibly small print underneath. *"For the avoidance of doubt, wishes cannot be revoked. Think carefully about consequences – wishes can seriously damage your health."*

"Oh there's no need to worry about that stuff," said her godmother in a silky voice. "It almost never goes completely wrong."

"Is that supposed to be comforting?" Isabella turned the paper around in her hands and looking thoughtful. "Who is the Guild of Fairy Godmothers?"

"Our 'governing' body," said her godmother proudly.

"Could I report you for failing in your duties?" Suddenly Isabella saw an opportunity.

"Yes, in theory," her fairy godmother sounded alarmed and then back in her silky tones added "but you wouldn't want to do that, particularly not now I'm granting you three, almost failsafe, wishes."

Isabella's legal training had not been completely wasted and she put it to use. "Here's the deal. If you grant my three wishes, without any undue side effects, I won't report you to your governing body."

"That you could even think I deserved it." Isabella's fairy godmother showed mock hurt. "Darling, it's a deal. To make your wishes just call the number on the bottom of the card. It's a premium rate line, but you shouldn't be on too long." With that, she got up. "Well I must dash, places to be, people to see. Good luck, darling." And she was gone.

"There's no time like the present," said Isabella to no one in particular and picked up her mobile phone.

The number rang for two rings before a crisp, recorded voice said, "You are through to the Guild of Fairy Godmothers three wishes helpline. I am sorry, but all our godmothers are busy at the moment, please hold and you will be put through to the next available godmother." Just as Isabella was about to hang up there was a click and a sing-song voice saying, "Hello, three wishes helpline, how may I be of service?"

"Hello, this is Isabella and I have been granted the use of three wishes by my fairy godmother. I would like..."

"Can you give me the reference number at the bottom? We need to make sure you are a genuine caller, it's a security check, you can never be too careful." The fairy godmother giggled.

"WISH4U2013." Isabella sounded a little impatient.

"That seems to be in order. Please tell me all three wishes."

"You mean I have to make them all at once? I can't wait to see how the first one turns out before choosing the second?" The caution on the card had left quite an impression and she was hoping for some sort of safety net.

"All three I'm afraid. You only get one call to the helpline."

It wasn't that Isabella didn't know what to wish for, that was clear in her mind, but she wasn't sure how to word them to avoid misunderstandings. "I wish for a prince of my own, to marry and live with, happily ever after."

"Is that all three wishes?" asked the godmother.

"That's the first wish," said Isabella firmly.

"Generally getting your prince, marrying him and living happily ever after would be seen as three separate wishes," said the helpline godmother.

"That is number one," repeated Isabella. "Wish number two, I've always wanted a perfect dog, as a companion and for number three I'd like you to straighten out my smile."

"That's a lot to wish for," said the godmother. "You're sure you wouldn't settle for the prince?"

"I knew it was too good to be true. You people have let me down quite enough already. Don't bother. Goodbye."

"No, please wait," the godmother sounded frantic. "I'll be in awful trouble for upsetting a caller. Let me just make sure I've written these three wishes down correctly and I'll see what I can do. There's so much to do. I really can't promise overnight success."

"I understand," said Isabella, the argument knocked out of her. "I'll be grateful for anything."

Isabella closed the phone and returned to her wine. She poured a second glass from the carafe and after taking in the brightly coloured buildings with their contrasting shutters, she closed her eyes, relaxing in the sunshine, listening to the hubbub of the market place around her. She could smell the scents from the flower market drifting on the breeze and at last began to unwind.

"Excuse me, is anyone sitting here?" A small, rather oddly pitched voice disturbed her reverie.

"No, it's free." She opened her eyes to see a scruffy looking puppy, clambering onto the chair. Her draw dropped open.

"When you're a stray, people pay less attention if you attach yourself to a human." He scratched vigorously. "You couldn't get a bowl of water for me could you?"

Isabella shook her head in disbelief. There was something about the little fellow that was endearing. Despite the obvious flea infestation, he had adorable brown eyes and a cheerful expression. His coat was curly and fawn, with patches of white. Isabella called the waiter and asked for some water.

"Thanks," he said, after the waiter had gone. "I'm Zed. Who are you?"

Isabella wasn't in the habit of talking to animals, but it was that sort of day. "Isabella. Zed's an odd name."

"I was Mum's twenty-sixth puppy. She'd run out of names by my turn. To be exact she ran out of names for my younger brother. Could've been worse; my eldest brother's called Elle. He comes in for some stick."

"Are you a prince and I'm supposed to kiss you?" Asked Isabella hesitantly.

"You've been reading too many fairy stories. That's frogs, though I'm game if you are. I'm your traditional stray. I left home when they couldn't feed me. Could you pass that bowl of peanuts down here?"

Isabella passed the peanuts and went back to her wine. They sat in silence and then finishing her drink and leaving money on the table, Isabella got up. "It was nice meeting you, but I'd best be going."

"Going," said Zed disappointed. "I've only just sat

down. My feet are killing me."

"You could stay here. I didn't expect you to come with me."

"Oh that's nice that is. I overhear you wishing for a dog and I think 'Zed my boy, your luck has changed. You can be the perfect faithful friend to this lovely lady'. So I present myself and now you say you're going."

"No offence, but I had in mind a pedigree dog, well-groomed without fleas."

"We're getting personal now. Well you're not a complete beauty to have for an owner. We can get some powder for the fleas and I smarten up quite well given the chance. Go on, what is there to lose?"

Isabella remembered the warning on the card and groaned. "Ok, but it's strictly on a trial basis. Two weeks. If either one of us isn't happy we go our separate ways. Now let's find some flea powder." She walked away and Zed hopped down and trotted closely beside her.

After the pet shop, they walked down to the promenade and found a bench looking out over the Mediterranean. "You can see why they call it the Cote d'Azur," Isabella gazed at the wonderful blues, brilliant in the afternoon sun.

"No," said Zed, "not unless you lift me up so I can see too. It's more the Cote de Concrete Wall from where I'm looking."

Isabella lifted Zed onto the wall where he could have a good look. "Just stand still a minute." She shook flea powder over his coat. "That should do it."

"There was me thinking you were picking me up to be nice," said Zed as he was lifted back to ground level. He had a good scratch. "This stuff goes everywhere." He sneezed over Isabella's sandals. "Oops sorry."

They sat quietly together, Isabella starting to enjoy the

companionship and Zed practising adoring looks for his new mistress.

"Hello, stranger," a deep voice boomed. "Fancy seeing you here."

"Matt," Isabella shouted in delight and hugged the tall, broad figure who had joined her.

"Who's your friend?" Matt bent down to pat Zed. Zed stretched out languidly to maximise the areas that could be rubbed and stroked.

"Long story," said Isabella. "Is Katy here?"

Matt looked suddenly tired. "Katy left me. Would you believe she traded me in for a younger model? There was me thinking that was my job." He laughed without humour.

"I'm sorry," said Isabella.

"Starting again at our age is all a bit of a shock. How about you?"

Isabella filled Matt in on how her career was going, then about her lovely house and ended by saying, "so I couldn't be more fortunate."

"Then why look so miserable. And where does this little chap fit in?" He reached down and scratched Zed behind the ear, resulting in Zed making little 'ooing' noises.

Isabella's shoulders dropped. "You're right, I'm not happy. In fact, it's been pretty lonely really. This little chap," she said, sounding much softer towards Zed, "has attached himself to me. I've just bought some flea powder and a brush." She opened the bag to show a large number of pet essentials, some dog food and several toys and treats that proved she really did have a softer side.

"Where are you living?"

"Fortunately, this side of the Channel. I wouldn't be able to take him back into England without a passport."

The rest of the afternoon passed in happy banter, until Matt finally asked if Isabella was free for dinner.

"I'll meet you at the restaurant," Isabella said hugging Matt. Then she walked back towards her apartment feeling as light as air with Zed scurrying along at her heels.

"There you are," said Zed between puffs and pants.

"There I am what?"

"Your prince," said Zed, "the first of your wishes."

"Don't be silly. Matt's been a friend for years. There's nothing like that between us and besides princes are young and dashing and arrive on a white charger."

"I hate to disappoint you," said Zed, "but have you looked in the mirror lately? At your age princes tend to be second hand, slightly balding and limp onto the scene sporting some injury."

Isabella walked in silence thinking about what Zed had just said. Surely he couldn't be right. Wishes one and two weren't exactly what she had in mind, but they weren't bad outcomes.

It was shortly after Zed's trial period had expired that Isabella received a letter enclosing an appointment card. She read it through twice then slung it down on the table looking furious.

"Problem?" Zed climbed onto the chair and read the card. "Isn't that what you asked for?" He asked scratching his head.

"My teeth! I wanted my buck teeth sorted out to straighten my smile. I didn't want collagen implants in my lips so they wouldn't move. I don't want that sort of a straight smile!"

Zed looked up from where he was sitting and grinned. "You got the first two wishes; you could always ring and ask for a refund on the third."

SHADOWS OF THE PAST

His was the fourth name down as I looked at the page headed '6th September' in the Book of Remembrance at the crematorium. I knew the entry by heart, but read the words aloud, as though performing some sort of ritual. In a way, I suppose I was. 'James McCreedy, my darling husband. Love as always Iris.' I still felt numb as I looked at the page and there was always that same cool air and almost musty smell, tinged with the scent of flowers. The lighting wasn't bright in the Remembrance Room, adding to the impression of faded reverence.

It meant two changes of bus to get here, since the timetable altered last June, but every year for the last eight, I made the pilgrimage and as long as God keeps me on this damned earth, I'm not going to let the bus company stop me spending these precious moments with my Jim. That was what it came down to, forty years of marriage reduced to an annual visit, to a single line on a page. I hadn't got anything else to live for. So, each year I had 364 days of waiting and then one brief moment to remember. Then it was gone, until the next year. Of course, I thought of him at other times but somehow it was different here. Here he still felt near enough to touch; near enough to talk to.

I replaced my handkerchief in my bag and clipped it shut. Then after adjusting my headscarf, I walked with frustrating, arthritic steps back towards the bus stop. There were forty-five minutes to wait in Richmond for the connecting bus. I decided a cup of tea would be in order. I looked at the youngsters in Starbucks, drinking from their mugs as I made my way towards Dickens and Jones. The young people looked vibrant and full of life, just as we did all those years ago. What days we had. With not having been able to have children of our own, there was little about today's youth I could identify with, except that feeling of being alive. I could still remember that. I could still remember the dances; Tea Dances we called them in my day. I could still remember the energy of falling in love with my Jim, but it was a distant and fading memory.

I bought my tea at the counter and took it to a table near the window. I was more comfortable with the formality and the protocol there than with the atmosphere of a modern coffee shop. Even then I would prefer to be served at my table, as they did in the old days. I was lost in thought, idly moving my cup round on its saucer.

"Do you mind if I join you?"

I was so far away with my memories that I said "No" automatically, without so much as looking up. I suppose I presumed the other tables were full. I was lost in a world of my own thoughts, a world that still belonged to my Jim.

"We were like that once, young, carefree, enjoying life."

I looked back from the window and for the first time registered the gentleman sitting opposite. "I beg your pardon?" I replied.

"I'm sorry," he said, "I didn't mean to intrude. I thought you were looking at the people outside, rushing around with places to go. I said, we were like that once. I didn't mean to disturb you. I'm Percy. Percy Fielding." He held out a hand and I was left with no alternative but to shake it.

I reluctantly introduced myself, "Mrs McCreedy."

I was taken aback by the directness with which he

asked, "And what do your friends call you, Mrs McCreedy?"

"Iris," I replied before overcoming the surprise of the question.

He started apologising for being so intrusive, telling me that I had reminded him of his wife Dorothy who had died the previous year and he just felt he needed to talk to me. Before I knew it, I was telling him about Jim. I don't think either of us was really listening to what the other was saying, it just felt better to have told someone. The time for my bus came and went but there was always another one.

Eventually he got up to leave and asked if he could escort me somewhere. It was a long time since I had been 'escorted' anywhere; the word had a lovely ring to it.

"I don't think so, thank you." I replied letting etiquette distance me from life again.

"Can I meet you again?" His neatly trimmed moustache wrinkled as he smiled.

My stiffness returned and I said, "I don't think so." But as he walked away I found myself saying, "I'm usually here on Wednesdays." I said no more than that, no time, nothing definite, surely that couldn't be wrong. Surely my Jim couldn't mind that.

The following Wednesday I wasn't feeling myself and didn't go into town. It was two weeks later when I next went. I didn't suppose for a minute that Percy would be there and took my tea to a table in a quiet corner.

It was then I heard a clearing of the throat and, "Do you mind if I join you, Mrs McCreedy?"

I knew I shouldn't, but I found myself smiling for the first time in ages and then immediately felt guilty, "Whatever would Jim think?"

But rather than picking up on my discomfort, Percy

replied in a conspiratorial voice, "Or my Dorothy." And we laughed like two naughty children that could be caught at any time. I don't remember the last time I had laughed so openly. Once again he sat and talked about Dorothy and I sat and talked about Jim and for an hour the world didn't seem so bad. Little by little over the coming Wednesdays he started to open up to me about how hard he found it on his own. He told me about his childhood in Sussex and how he'd moved here in the 60's when his children were in their teens. Both his son and his daughter were living abroad now, one in France and the other in America. He proudly showed me pictures of his grandchildren. He loved the time we spent together on a Wednesday and I found it was infectious and I started to lower my guard a little. We met like that for about three months, nothing more. We didn't exchange telephone numbers or addresses; we just met for our Wednesday tea and coffee. Then he asked if I would like to join him for lunch. I wasn't sure I should do that, what would Jim think and he reminded me of that Wednesday when we had laughed so much, having reacted as though we were having an affair, rather than two people alone in the world.

By February, we were meeting twice a week; then in April, we went out for a whole day together. It's odd finding you don't stop getting butterflies, even at my age.

As we walked down to the river one day in July, Percy stopped and said, "Mrs McCreedy." I always know it's something special now when he calls me that. "Mrs McCreedy, I know I haven't got much to offer and we may not be on this earth much longer, but do you think you would do me the great honour to be my wife?" He didn't do anything silly, like get down on one knee. He would never have managed to get up again. Even so, I wasn't expecting it.

I was so shocked. I told him I needed time to think about it, but what I really thought was, it wasn't right and that Jim would mind dreadfully.

I didn't go for a cup of tea that Wednesday or the one after that. I didn't think I could face seeing him. By the third week, I was so desperately unhappy. It felt as though Jim had died all over again. In a way, he had. Strangely, when I was with Percy I could talk about Jim and he was more alive to me then, than at any other time. Would it really be so wrong to marry someone else? I wished more than ever that I had children I could talk to about it, but life had never been that generous to me. I went for tea that day and there was Percy waiting patiently. I didn't know what to say to him so we just talked as we used to, he about Dorothy and me about Jim.

As I got up to go, I simply said, "Could we ask Jim's permission?" Percy's beaming smile said it all. It was settled. Percy would come with me in a couple of weeks' time on my annual visit to the crematorium.

It was strange sharing the bus with someone on the 6th of September this year, but not unpleasantly so. Somehow, the crematorium seemed brighter than I remembered it. Silently we stood side by side. As the tears flowed down my cheeks, I quietly asked Jim if he would understand.

Ever so gently, Percy took my hand in his and in a voice much stronger than my own said, "I promise to take good care of her for you, just as long as I can." Then he put his arm around my shoulder and I felt the warmth of a new beginning and the continuity of love. "Shall we go, Mrs McCreedy?" Then turning back to the Book of Remembrance, he said "Farewell, Jim, until next year."

THE WALL OF SHOES

"Don't stand on ceremony, come through. I was just putting the kettle on. If I can find it amongst this lot." Elsie laughed as she led Anne and Sylvia through to the kitchen.

"We just wanted to welcome you to Highfield Close. It's a very nice area. We do hope you'll fit in." Anne looked sternly at Sylvia who held out the flowers to their new neighbour.

"That's very kind of you both, thank you. Moving hasn't been nearly as bad as I was expecting. My friend Terry offered to move my belongings in his van." Elsie smiled as a large man with tattoos on his upper arms carried a mixture of suitcases and boxes past them into the lounge.

Anne frowned as her eyes followed Terry. "We do have a neighbourhood watch scheme and of course there's the residents' committee." She began arranging the flowers into a vase on the side.

"Oh you really don't need to do that. I think Gina was rather looking forward to sorting things out for me." Elsie winked at Gina. "Why don't you two ladies bring your cups of tea and come and sit down while Gina gets on?"

Gina was a girl of nineteen. She was there with her toddler Bethany. Elsie settled her elegant frame in the high-backed chair and started explaining to Gina exactly where she would like everything put.

"What about the shoes?" Gina asked as Bethany picked up a bright pink shoe with a three-inch heel and big frilly bow.

"Oh dear, I really do need some shelves. You'll have to leave them there for the time being, dear." Elsie smiled.

Gina put the steel toe-capped boots along the foot of the wall, next to a trendy pair of trainers. Then she put the highly polished black patent leather pair and the pink ones that Bethany was holding on the end of the line. She continued to work her way neatly along the wall with the tiny first pair of shoes of a child, the ballet shoes, the riding boots and strappy sandals. Sylvia sat on the settee and watched, while Anne sat in the chair near the window.

"And not a single pair in my size." Elsie chuckled to herself.

"Well!" said Anne getting up. "There's a young hoodlum coming down your path. I'll soon sort him out."

"Oh please sit down, Anne." She looked across at the high-tech training shoes. "That will be Craig. He won't bite." Elsie turned to Gina, "Would you mind letting him in dear?"

"We don't normally have youths who look like that in Highfield Close. I think we'd best be off. Come along Sylvia." Anne bustled towards the door, tripping over a pair of men's brogues as she went and hitting her arm against the door frame.

She tutted. "These are a dreadful hazard. I can't see what you want with them."

Sylvia gave a weak smile and followed, being careful to avoid the shoes.

They were barely through the door when Elsie heard Anne saying, "And I was expecting a respectable type of woman, not one who mixed with riffraff. What about those ridiculous shoes? A fruitcake that's what she is. I'd probably best not invite her to our summer barbecue. I've a good mind to get the residents' committee to send a letter of complaint."

As Elsie went back to her chair, she looked sadly at the highly polished patent court shoes with their pointed toes and uncomfortable heels.

Elsie's day was filled with visitors and by the middle of the afternoon she was starting to feel quite settled. For the first time in the day she was on her own and she stood back to admire her new home. There was a tap at the front door. To Elsie's surprise, it was Sylvia. "On your own this time?"

"Do you mind if I come in?"

Elsie led the way into the lounge. "Come and sit down."

"I was just wondering," said Sylvia twisting her sleeve between her fingers.

Elsie smiled in encouragement.

"I was just wondering about the shoes."

"You mean that unlike Anne, you think there may be a reason rather than pure eccentricity." She grinned.

Sylvia nodded. "I wanted to apologise for her outburst earlier too. She can be a bit..."

Elsie held up her hand before Sylvia could say any more. "My mother always told me that before you criticise another person you should walk a mile in their shoes. It's not always possible to do that literally, so I do it in my head. I bought all the shoes to help me. When Anne said she thought I was a fruitcake earlier I came in here and looked at those court shoes and I walked me a mile of Anne's life. I thought about how hard she must work for all the rest of us residents and how little thanks she probably gets."

Sylvia was looking confused. "And all your visitors?"

"They are all people I've walked a mile with. Gina was a teenage mum who used to sit on the bench outside my house, rocking Bethany in her pram. She'd got nowhere else to go. Her mum wouldn't let her stay around the house and there was no one to look after the baby, so she'd just sit there for hours. One day when it started raining, I asked Gina if she'd like to come inside and have a cup of tea. We've been friends ever since."

"What about the man who moved you in?"

"Terry," said Elsie looking at the workman's boots. "He came to fix a leaky roof for me. His Mum had just died of cancer. He wasn't really concentrating on his work and managed to cut through a water pipe. We sat and talked while he waited for the emergency plumber to come and fix it. He was having a rough time and as a builder he couldn't really say anything to his workmates. It didn't fit the image."

Sylvia picked up the brogues. "And the man I saw leaving a while ago?"

"I was in a queue in the bank and he was behind me. He was obviously agitated and something was wrong. He went to the till next to mine and he snapped at the clerk, so I said 'Excuse me, but can I buy you a cup of tea?' He was too shocked to say no. I took him into the teashop next door and listened to his story. He'd just been for a job interview. He'd been made redundant two months earlier and was desperately in need of work. He'd gone into the bank to see if there was enough money in his account to pay that month's mortgage payment. He's got a wife and three children that depend on him and he feels as though he's let them down."

Finally, Sylvia picked up the training shoe.

"Craig," said Elsie. "He was loitering outside my house, kicking the wall. He doesn't get on with his step-dad. The only place he'd got was street corners and he was starting to earn a reputation for getting into trouble. He started coming round every day after school to talk to me and we even started doing his homework together. It was the first time anyone had really taken an interest in him." Elsie sat back. "So that tells you about the shoes. Terry's coming round tomorrow afternoon to put some shelves up for me so that no one else trips over them."

Sylvia nodded, a tear escaping from the corner of her eye. "You know, Elsie," she said, getting up. "I think you may be the sanest one in this close. If you're free, I'd like you to come to the barbecue next Saturday as my guest and when I get home, I'm going to start my very own wall of shoes."

ABOUT THE AUTHOR

Rosemary J Kind writes because she has to. You could take almost anything away from her except her pen and paper. Failing to stop after the book that everyone has in them, she has gone on to publish books in both non-fiction and fiction, the latter including novels, humour, short stories and poetry. She also regularly produces magazine articles in a number of areas and writes regularly for the dog press. As a child she was desolate when, at the age of ten, her then teacher would not believe that her poem based on *Stig of the Dump* was her own work and she stopped writing poetry for several years as a result. She was persuaded to continue by the invitation to earn a little extra pocket money by 'assisting' others to produce the required poems for English homework!

Always one to spot an opportunity, she started school newspapers and went on to begin providing paid copy to her local newspaper at the age of sixteen.

For twenty years she followed a traditional business career, before seeing the error of her ways and leaving it all behind to pursue her writing full-time.

She spends her life discussing her plots with the characters in her head and her faithful dogs, who always put the opposing arguments when there are choices to be made.

Always willing to take on challenges that sensible people regard as impossible, she set up the short story download site Alfie Dog Fiction which she ran for six years. During that time it grew to become one of the largest short story download sites in the world, representing over 300 authors and carrying over 1600 short stories. Her hobby is developing the Entlebucher Mountain Dog in the UK and when she brought her beloved Alfie back from Belgium he was only the tenth in the country.

She started writing *Alfie's Diary* as an internet blog the day Alfie arrived to live with her, intending to continue for a year or two. Twelve years later it goes from strength to strength and has been repeatedly named as one of the top ten dog blogs in the UK.

For more details about the author please visit her website at www.rjkind.co.uk For more details about her dogs then you're better visiting www.alfiedog.me.uk

OTHER BOOKS BY ROSEMARY J. KIND

The Appearance of Truth

Lisa Forster's birth certificate belonged to a baby who died. Her apparently happy upbringing was a myth and her parents had a dark secret.

With Pete Laundon's help Lisa sets about searching for the truth. She follows up all possible routes, until with no options left she goes to the newspapers for help. After 30 years, who if anyone knows: Who is Lisa Forster? Why was she never told? And who was the baby who died?

The Appearance of Truth is the gripping tale of one woman's search for identity.

New York Orphan

From fleeing the Irish Potato Famine, to losing his parents on the ship to New York, seven-year-old Daniel Flynn knows about adversity. As Daniel sings the songs of home to earn pennies for food, pick-pocket Thomas Reilly becomes his ally and friend, until he too is cast out onto the street.

A destitute refugee in a foreign land, Daniel, together with Thomas and his sister Molly, are swept up by the Orphan Train Movement to find better lives with families across America. For Daniel will the dream prove elusive?

How strong are bonds of loyalty when everything is at stake?

Based on real history, the strength of the characters in New York Orphan will move you with their desperate plight to survive. A gripping story of love, loss, betrayal and bonds of kinship.

The Lifetracer

A death threat. An inexperienced private eye. Now his young son is in danger.

Connor Bancroft is one of life's good guys, but he's more used to dealing with infidelity than murder. Now someone has sent a countdown clock showing 'Time to Death'. The police won't take it seriously and Connor is called in to investigate. Soon other connected murders come to light and Connor tries to piece the case together.

As the clock is ticking down, Connor is unwittingly drawn into a complex story of revenge, but he is nowhere close to finding who sent the threat.

If you like rooting for an underdog, then you'll love this book. Connor is struggling. Now Mikey, his eight-year-old son, is at risk and time is running out. – Can Connor find who's behind the murders before it's too late?

Who is the Lifetracer?

Buy this book today and find out if Connor can save his son.

Alfie's Woods

Alfie is fascinated when Hedgehog is recaptured following his escape from the Woodland Prison. Too young to understand money laundering, Alfie assumes that Hedgehog should be given sympathy for washing his money.

Hedgehog, overwhelmed that any other creature should care about him, finds the strength to change his life. As an ex-convict, Hedgehog meets with opposition at every step and it is only the faith of his friends and their unwavering support that enables him to turn his life round.

Alfie's Woods is a story of the power of friendship and the difference it can make to all of us.

Lovers Take up Less Space

Lovers Take up Less Space is a humorous review of the addictive misery of commuting on London Underground. A blow by blow account of everything from how to find breathing space on a packed Tube train, to the psychological torture of passengers eating a fresh hot bag of chips and not passing them round. It includes games to transform underground travel from a necessary evil to a recreational activity, together with surprising facts and figures answering questions you had not yet thought to ask.

Pet Dogs Democratic Party Manifesto

PDDP manifesto is a humorous look at key political issues from a dog's point of view. Alfie Dog is a self-styled political leader who believes that for too long pets have been seen as the underdogs, working tirelessly for little more than a pat on the head. He believes it is time for the country to go to the dogs literally instead of metaphorically; for the prejudice dogs face to be swept aside; time to vote for a more equal and just society.

Alfie's Diary

An entertaining and thought provoking dog's eye view of the world. His unique blend of observational humour and satire enables him to highlight the peculiarities of humans and comment on their idiosyncrasies. Behind all of this Alfie talks about all the normal processes of growing up and the insecurities and emotions faced by any young puppy. Through his revelations, his humour and his pathos, Alfie will make you laugh and at times make you cry.

From Story Idea to Reader
Whether brushing up your writing skills or starting out, this book will take you through the whole process from inspiration to conclusion.
Are you looking to submit your work for publication, enter a competition, or do you want to self-publish? This practical guide will help you every step of the way.
Between them, Patsy Collins and Rosemary J. Kind have sold hundreds of short stories, written more than twenty published books and produced numerous articles for Writing Magazine and similar publications. They've both judged writing competitions and run workshops, and Rosemary has read and edited thousands of short stories and published dozens of books for other writers.
With the information, help and encouragement in this book, you too could see your work in print.
Buy it now and give your writing life a boost.

The Complete Entlebucher Mountain Dog Book
This book provides a complete insight into the Entlebucher Mountain Dog. Whether you are looking to add an Entlebucher to your family, get the best out of your relationship with a dog you already own or are interested in the story of the breed itself and its development in the UK, this is the book for you.
Illustrated with over 160 colour photographs, The Complete Entlebucher Mountain Dog Book will charm, educate and delight everyone who has a soft spot in their hearts for dogs of this or any breed.

This authoritative guide will help you to understand how to train your Entlebucher before he trains you and how to get the best out of your relationship with this wonderful breed.

Poems for Life

A collection of poems by prize winning poet Rosemary J. Kind, including the inspirational 'Carpe Diem'. Published to raise money for Age UK, all profits will go to support their work.

Rosemary's work has appeared in a wide range of publications including Hand Luggage Only, England's Standard, The Leicester Mercury, The Methodist Recorder, Cooldog Publications and many others. Her work provides inspiration and at times much humour. Her style is easily accessible and will strike notes of recognition in many readers.

Alfie Dog Fiction

Taking your imagination for a walk

Visit our website at www.alfiedog.com

Join us on Facebook
http://www.facebook.com/AlfieDogLimited